The Clam before the Storm

and other writing

John Griffiths

First published in Great Britain by Grenadier Productions and Publications, 5 St. Helens Drive, Hove, Sussex BN3 8EA

www.grenadierpp.com

A CIP catalogue record for this book is available from the British Library

ISBN 978-1-902000-05-3

www.e-griff.com

Acknowledgements

I offer my sincere and grateful thanks to all the keen and supportive writers on the UKAuthors.com website who between them helped me refine many of these pieces. In particular I would like to mention Aliya Whiteley and David Gardiner.

My biggest thanks go to C R Krishnan (Chris), whose goodwill made this book possible.

Foreword

I have invented stories all my life, but only in the last few years have I had the time to write them down in good order. True writing is something that stirs the emotions, makes the reader think, and my hope is that you will find your own examples here – as well as occasional patches of humour.

This collection is a personal trip though my world. There is no strict categorisation, no one style in my writing. I explore. This book is to dip into and taste, maybe to read something you would not normally choose, but perhaps find you enjoy.

I also write under the pen-name 'Posy', who has her own identity as Petra Barrow, from Fife. Many of the poems are hers. You may recognise her voice.

So, here is some of my work.

Note: In the contents list, poems are shown in italics. Also, stories with an obvious US setting use American English spellings.

Contents

The Clam before the Storm

and other writing

The Clam before the Storm

an aperitif

It's the clam before the storm!
I gulp it quickly,
Watching the approaching hammerheads on the horizon,
Washing it down with a fine wine,
Before boarding up
And going inside.

The Night Wind

Creature of earth and moonlight,
She rides the west wind,
Warm as a lover's breath
Above the soughing wood.

Rises to the mordant gloom,
Drops landward to the prey.
Then beats a strong tattoo,
A weighty retreat.

Midnight. On the air,
A peaking cry.
She is near,
Attending to the business of the night.

Noon

Through the eyes of an innocent …

I'm sure Mr Sigournis must be very large, even for a man. I don't mean large looking up, but large going round. He seems to have places where other people don't.

We're on the porch, Mrs Sigournis and I, in the shade. Mr Sigournis is mowing the lawn, or trying to. It's a lovely sight, the wide lawn, the trees behind, the bright sky as the backdrop. The mower leaves a trail on the grass that looks lighter than the rest. Mr Sigournis is a vast blot on this vista. He wears shorts and a big, billowy white shirt. His face is dark. That is bad, his face is usually pale. His veins are standing out and his eyes are bulging.

Mrs Sigournis is drinking iced lemonade. She has a small plate of biscuits on a tray. She is knitting. Occasionally she smiles at Mr Sigournis, but he never notices. She wears light clothes, she looks cool. Her skin is pale. She is in a rocking chair and moves slightly. The overhead fan wafts cool air over us. I stay still. Maybe she will give me one of her biscuits? If I ask nicely. She is kind. And there are plenty of biscuits.

The sun is high. Noon is hot. Mr Sigournis always starts to mow the lawn at noon. Mrs Sigournis 'tut-tuts' every time, but it makes no difference. Mr Sigournis likes to mow the lawn *before* lunch. Lunch is at two. Ella prepares it. Ella is kind. She is kind to me, like Mrs Sigournis. She has time for me. Mr Sigournis does not. I am Mrs Sigournis's baby, but I am not his. This can be upsetting.

'Carl, come take an iced drink!'

Mr Sigournis waves his hand dismissively. He is looking at the mower. If he is to complete the mowing before lunch, he must 'get on'. I've heard him say those words: 'get on'. Now he has a big metal box, and he is taking shiny things out and clanging and pushing them on parts of the mower. His mouth is open and gasping, his face runs sleek with wetness. His white shirt is grey in places where it sticks to him. Soon he stands up and pushes the mower again, disappearing from our sight.

Mrs Sigournis turns back to her knitting, shaking her head. She has a pleasant smile. She is a kind mother. I decide to try for a biscuit; I get up and go over to her. I wait until she notices me, then ask politely. She laughs, reaches for the plate, and gives me *two*. I don't push my luck. I accept them and walk over to the bushes to find a shady place to sit down.

I can see Mr Sigournis again. He is making loud noises; he is hitting the lawnmower, just like the times he hit me. I take my biscuits somewhere else.

The sun is still high. I wander back to Mrs Sigournis, and sit beside her on the porch.

'Where's Mr Sigournis?' she asks. I don't answer. I just stare at her. She smiles at me and her eyes twinkle. 'Never mind,' she says.

Mrs Sigournis is worried, I can tell. She is shouting, 'Carl, Carl, where are you?' He does not reply. Last time I saw him he was lying down, resting. I think that's the best thing. The sun is so hot at noon, you should keep in the shade. He is in the shade now.

His eyes were opening and closing and he reached out his

hand to me. I was concerned for him. This was not how he normally behaved. I thought that perhaps I should call Mrs Sigournis. But last time I did, he shouted and hit me. So I didn't. He appeared to be resting. His face had changed to pale. That's better, I thought. Mrs Sigournis used to tell me, 'He's not supposed to get so worked up, look at his blood pressure.' I have learned many words. Some I do not understand, but I know their mood, I know which are bad.

Mr Sigournis is lying behind the bushes. His face is pale, that is good. He is very still, that is good. His eyes are open, and he did not blink when I licked them. That is unusual. Maybe it is bad. I can't tell.

Lunch will be ready soon. Ella will give me something. Something left over.

Well

When I wrote this along with a few other 'dark' poems, some were convinced I was about to give it all up. I didn't.

Hot afternoon, July,
Beneath a blazing sky,
I do not question why
The well is dry.

A pen in my right hand,
No words at my command,
That's how I understand:
The well is dry.

I think upon my life,
My children and my wife,
I'm tired of all the strife.
My well is dry.

Minna

Some of my fiercest critics love this story, others say it is 'thin and empty' – but then, I meant it to be.

Minna stacked the used trays on the rack in the bakery then selected some fancy cakes: pink icing, hundreds and thousands, little twirls of cream; she could almost taste them.

The tinkle of the bell took her back into the shop. Mrs Dennie never said much. With a muttered greeting, she dropped the correct change onto Minna's hand and hurried out. Minna stared at the bright coins as they glinted in the reflections from the bevelled glass of the door, reminding her of the fish in the loch. She and Will used to watch the silver, sliding shapes, just under the surface. Why did she not walk there any more? Too busy, Minna shrugged. She sorted the coins into the till. For the umpteenth time, she read the words on the shop window. She liked to practice. The back-to-front 'Archie' was easy, as were 'Mowat' and 'Baker' but she still found 'Confectioner' difficult – so silly!

Minna smiled to herself and glanced at the clock: nine-thirty. Shaped like a loaf, it had graced the shop for over twenty years. Nearly as long as me, she thought wryly. The plastic notice hanging on the glass door proclaimed 'Open' to any passer-by, but on her side it said 'Closed'. Through the glass lay the single main street of the town, lined with stone houses. The street ended at the chapel, behind which rose a hillside, steep and dark with sheep scattered in aimless patterns about its looming flank.

She decided to clean the glass shelves and mirrors. Taking the cloth from under the counter, she began to wipe methodically, a task she carried out at regular intervals throughout the day.

The bell tinkled. She turned.

'Morning, Minna!'

'Oh, good morning Mr Duncan, how are you?'

'Fine.' Mr Duncan smiled, ducking his head to view the sky over the hill through the door. 'But we'll have some rain this afternoon, I've a feeling.' Minna nodded as she served him, acknowledging his words. The bell tinkled again and she watched him walk away down the street. Rain, eh? Pity. She went back to wiping the shelves.

A noise from the bedroom above told her Archie was turning over in his sleep. She looked at the clock. Ten o'clock. Yes – he was usually restless now but always slept through to the afternoon.

Twenty-five past … Mrs Banner would be in soon. She wasn't comfortable with Mrs Banner, perhaps because of Will. He had introduced her as 'Stephanie', but these days Minna was more formal. She had nearly been to see her after Will had gone, but there was no hope of closeness between them after Mrs Banner forbade Will to walk to chapel with Minna on Sunday as they had done since they were teenagers, because 'people would talk'. Talk! Minna thought angrily. Their eldest boy took after Will. When he was small and came in for a loaf, she would give him a cake and pay for it herself. She used to love seeing his eyes light up and his face break into a smile exactly like Will's.

At the funeral, she'd sat at the back so people wouldn't 'talk'. They had said some nice things about Will. When she left, Stephanie had said, 'Thank you for coming, Minna.' Thank you for coming! Remembering that day, her eyes filled with tears. She pulled out a tissue and dabbed her eyes.

The bell tinkled. Mrs Banner stepped into the shop.

'Morning, Minna! The usual, please.' Minna fetched a wholemeal loaf and carefully wrapped it in the thin white paper. She loved the paper, every sheet so clean, so new and fresh, crackling under her fingers. She placed the wrapped loaf on the counter.

'Anything else?' she enquired. 'Some cakes for the boys?'

Mrs Banner laughed. 'Boys, Minna? They don't eat cakes any more, dear. Jason's off to University soon.'

Jason, what kind of name was that? She remembered the time Will had told her about it: 'Well, Minna, Stephanie likes it and that's good enough for me.' And so it was. That was one of the things she'd admired about him.

'Minna?' Mrs Banner's voice interrupted her thoughts.

'Oh, that's a shame,' Minna said. 'Och, he's such a cheerful soul. He makes me smile.'

Mrs Banner looked thoughtful. 'Minna dear, we've all got to move on, you know.' Minna was not sure what she meant.

'On your account then, Mrs Banner?'

'Yes, thank you, dear. You take care of yourself.' The bell tinkled. She was gone.

Will had once said he'd take care of her. He was always very serious about things like that. It was after she'd been dumped by Charlie Greig. She was so miserable but when Will had said he'd take care of her, she laughed. She felt sorry after, she thought she might have hurt his feelings, but he'd never said anything.

Five to eleven: time was getting on. She went into the back, filled the kettle at the sink and plugged it in. She lifted down the tray with the tea things and placed it on the table. She loved her special cup: porcelain, gold-rimmed with red and yellow flowers on the sides, lip delicately fluted, so the tea flowed over the thinnest of china as she drank. Just the feel on her lower lip was a pleasure. The teapot and cup were part of a set. Several cups and plates had been broken over the years but she had been lucky with the pot. Minna filled it, stirred, replaced the lid. She was alert for the shop door but it was unusual for anyone to come in at this time, except a passing motorist in search of a snack.

They'd started doing sandwiches a few years ago. It was her idea. Mrs McGilvray had been horrified. 'Who on earth would pay good money for something you can make yourself?' Minna suggested people didn't have the time. The old woman looked at her over her glasses. 'Now, Minna, just remember you can always find time for the things that really matter, my dear.' She had died a few years ago but Minna still recalled her words.

Taking her purse and plate, she went to the shop, selected a cake and paid before carrying it to the back room. She sipped the tea and nibbled the cake. When young, she had gobbled cakes. Will chided her for it. 'A good, steady boy' her parents said. Too steady, she'd thought then. She remembered that day they'd sat in this room together:

'I'll miss you lots, Will,' she said through a mouthful of cake.

'Careful!' He brushed the sprayed crumbs off his trousers. 'These are my best clothes.'

'I know,' Minna said, giggling. 'What are you going for?'

'Final interview,' Will replied.

'You're so clever, Will.'

'So are you Minna. You know that. Why did you leave?'

'I was bored at school, Will, I want some excitement.'

'In a shop?'

She was surprised. Will was usually so careful and polite.

'Only for now, Will. I'm going to do things, make something of my life, travel the world and sip champagne by the ocean.' Will laughed. She always made him laugh when she talked like that.

'And marry a millionaire I bet!'

'Yes, someone who is fun.' She stressed the last word.

'Better than the types you go out with here, then.'

Again! This was not like Will.

'Don't you criticise my friends, Will Banner. You're just jealous 'cos you haven't got a car like Pete.' Pete was Minna's latest, a car salesman from the town. She did not know what had got into Will. She didn't have time for this nonsense. 'I'm not listening to all this again Will. I'm not staying here and being dull all my life. You are my best friend, Will. That's all. Don't make me angry!'

Will had jumped up. She never knew what he intended to do. Try to kiss her again? That could have been exciting. But his arm caught his cup and sent it flying, crashing to the floor. Immediately, he was calm, apologetic, sweeping up the pieces and putting them in the bin. Then the bell tinkled and she'd had to go into the shop. After the customer left, Will emerged and made for the door.

'Wish me luck, Minna.'

'Best of luck, Will.' She smiled at him as he stood in the doorway. It was the end of summer and the hillside behind him was darkening. He stood for a moment, framed against the houses and the hill, as if he was about to say something. Then he turned, and was gone. The bell tinkled and the plastic sign swung from side to side. 'Closed,' it said.

They'd never sat in the back room again. She saw him when he came home, of course. They walked together, when he had time. The next year, he brought Stephanie back for a visit. She was from England. He'd been there. He told Minna all about London. 'I want you two to be the best of friends,' he said as he introduced them. The two girls smiled politely.

Minna had tired of 'fun' quickly enough. Various 'Petes' came and went. False laughter and fumbling in the back of motorcars had palled. She had tried to find more steady relationships but her mother's long final illness stole her youth. Her father passed away soon after. She did not begrudge them. They'd done everything for her. They'd saved to send her to university and had been bitterly disappointed when she left school early, she realised belatedly. At first she thought of spending some of the money they left to her on a world tour – to visit the places she dreamed of. But she didn't fancy going alone. She was a bit old for all that, she told herself, and besides, she couldn't afford the time away.

The bell tinkled. Minna jumped up, dropping her cup. The last one. She could not believe it. The pieces lay on the floor. She remembered standing there with Will, that time so long ago. Then she was crying, really crying! Tears streamed down her cheeks and she was sobbing. The bell tinkled again. Minna ran into the shop, heedless of her appearance. Whoever it was had gone. A loaf was missing and coins lay on the counter. Mrs Murray, she thought, mentally reviewing her list of customers. This wouldn't do. She looked up at the clock. Quarter past eleven. Must get on! She went out to the washroom, washed her face and patted her cheeks dry and brushed her hair. Then she returned and swept up the pieces of the broken cup, holding back the welling tears.

At eleven-thirty the shop became busy, as usual, with two or three people at a time waiting to be served. Minna tended to each politely, never forgetting small enquiries about health, children and the latest gossip. She liked this part of the day, time seemed to fly.

Twelve-thirty. Things were slowing down. Minna cleared

the empty trays, transferred all the remaining cakes, tidied the loaves and wiped all the counters and shelves again. The shop closed for lunch at one and there were always a few last-minute stragglers. Finally, the last customer left and she set the latch and turned the sign round. Taking her time, she prepared a sandwich, fetched her purse from her coat in the back room, went to the till and paid. She carried the sandwich into the back room and placed the plate down on the table next to the tea-tray. There was a vacant space between the teapot and the milk jug and sugar bowl. No cup.

The bell did not tinkle all afternoon. At four, a creak on the stair heralded Archie Mowat's appearance.

'Minna! What are you doing here?'

'Just waiting to hand over, Mr Mowat.'

'But it's Wednesday, girl. Half-day. You should be at home. You need time to relax, enjoy yourself, not be stuck here.' He gave her the same look as Will had so long ago. Her eyes went to the pot, the uneaten sandwich and the space where the cup should be. Perhaps she could find another the same?

'Och, it's all right Mr Mowat. I've got plenty of time, really. All the time in the world.'

She rose, methodically tidied away the tea things, took off her coverall, donned her coat and hat, picked up her bag and said goodnight.

As Minna walked toward the glass door, she saw the hillside looming in the dusk against the black sky. It was raining. Summer had gone and autumn was following.

It'll be winter soon, she thought.

Brush

A poem written around the same time as 'The Night Wind'

Below the fell, the air is thickened black,
In night-time rendered with a bristling brush,
And through the gnarly boughs of waiting trees
The spirits fly forth in a prickling rush.

And now, the good have fled and all beside,
Across the hill and valley's depth they'll seek.
The cast of sin is wrought upon the land,
And evil come to persecute the meek.

When morning breaks the scene is bleak and bitter,
Men crying over children and their wives.
There is no hope, there is no rescue coming,
What's done is done, and nothing else survives.

Lucky Seven

Another of my small stories about small characters

'Please Missis.' Shuang stood at the door to the terrace.

'Yes, Shuang?' I turned towards her. It was raining outside. 'Are you dry out there?'

'Yes, Missis.' She waited.

'Do you want something?'

'Missis, a cup. Please.'

I looked at the frail seven-year old standing in my doorway, dark eyes fixed on me. I had taken her in after the earthquake. Her whole family had been killed. She wouldn't come in the house, except to the outer rooms, and would only sleep outside. For now, while the good weather lasted, a makeshift tent in my enclosed garden provided shelter and security. Later in the year we would have to see.

'What for?' I was curious.

'For Ai, Missis, to collect water for her.'

I pointed at the tap. 'There is water.' My house boasted a piped supply.

She shook her head. 'No, Missis, he needs fresh water. From the sky.' Her small hand raised upward, pointing.

I didn't argue. I had become used to Shuang's ways, her small, rigid beliefs: they seemed part of a defence mechanism for managing life and forgetting the disaster. The bird was part of it. I had tried to persuade her to let it free, but she said it was all she had. As she had lain in the rubble, the bird had alighted next to her and sung. It had saved her, she believed. I could not understand why the bird had stayed to be caught by one of the rescuers and placed in a bamboo cage, but Shuang was sure. 'Ai will stay with me as long as I live,' she had said.

I gave her an old cup, and she scampered off, placing the cup carefully on a stone, heedless of the rain. Then she went back to her shelter.

After all the problems back home and the break-up with John, I wanted a different life. I had studied China for years, and when the country started opening up five years ago, I found myself a dilapidated house in a small town in the country. It had been the home of a local party member, a dignitary. They have all gone to the cities now, to industry and wealth, as do many of the young, so our town consists mainly of older people. A young girl like Shuang is a rarity, and so is well received. Her good nature also helps. She does small tasks, fetching and carrying, which she pursues with diligence. In return, she receives gifts of food, clothes and coins. She helps me with tasks to earn her keep and brings the food she is given to me and we eat together.

In truth, I love her companionship. I have few visitors, and although the townsfolk are friendly, to them I believe I remain an outsider with strange habits. One of my few luxuries is internet access provided via satellite, and that has engendered a great deal of curiosity.

'But what is it for?' asked Xiang-Li, my neighbour, who had glimpsed the coloured screen through my window. 'Is it like a TV?' She pronounced it the western way, 'tee-vee', which sounded comical amidst the complex tones of the local dialect, reminding me of my native Wales and its many adopted words. I had tried to explain to her, but seemingly failed, possibly because finding word equivalents in Chinese was difficult. But no doubt my words were passed on to her circle of friends and beyond. I was a focus of interest. Sometimes I asked for things in the local grocery shop that raised eyebrows, but the proprietor there, who called herself Mrs Toy, soon cottoned onto the fact that I'd pay a premium for something special, and her diligence in searching out sources was remarkable. After a while, I noticed that instead of the one special package with my name on, there were often two or three others, and Mrs Toy was always ready to quiz me on how a certain vegetable might be used and what meat it would go with. Presumably such information was passed on to my growing circle of fans. The specialities were not even 'foreign' in the true sense, mostly Chinese, but were produce that was little known in our isolated region.

The landslip that buried Shuang's village, although triggered by an earthquake, was most likely the result of the massive earthworks and changes that had taken place around the new dams. Spoil had been dumped in heaps, watercourses changed, and the whole run-off of the rains had carved new gulleys and streams in the vicinity. It was the price of progress, I supposed.

Now it was the season of the Perseids, mid-August. Each night I sat out on the porch and gazed at the night sky, ablaze not only with stars, but also a silver rain of shooting stars. I would see the flickering candle in Shuang's tent extinguish as she settled herself to sleep.

Shuang would often invite me for tea. She was always a serious child, but on these occasions especially so. She would have a small fire burning outside her tent, on which a tin cauldron boiled. Since the time she had borrowed the cup from me for Ai, she had acquired a fine set of her own. She made the tea solemnly, and poured it out, offering a plate of sweets made of chestnut paste. I enjoyed these interludes.

Although we chattered and gossiped over our regular meals, here we spoke more seriously, about deeper things. She would talk about her family, her sisters and brothers, her friends.

'I am the only one spared,' she said. 'I should not have been spared. Heaven will take me one day.'

'You were lucky,' I told her, 'Make the most of your luck.'

'No,' she said, 'I am unlucky, very unlucky.'

I disliked this pessimistic talk, and tried to lighten the mood. I worried what was going on in her seven-year old mind.

Shuang would allow Ai to fly free in the tent. I was worried the bird might escape. Although I felt it should be free, I was concerned about Shuang's reaction should it do so.

'Do not worry,' she said as I fussed with the flap of cloth covering the doorway. 'She will not leave me.'

Shuang's candle went out and the garden was dark. The sky blazed. Almost at once, I was disturbed by a pattering sound, like rain. It was over as quickly as it had begun, and I could see no sign of wetness beyond the porch. I went out into the garden, and an insect stung my arm, so I hurried into the house. It was unusual to have insects this time of the season.

In the morning, I awoke to a bright sun. I realised I could not hear Shuang singing. I got up and looked out. The tent door was still pulled across. I slipped on a gown and walked over to Shuang's small space. For the first time I saw she had made a garden of her own in a flower bed – some herbs, some wild flowers grew. I smiled.

'Shuang!' I called. There was no answer, so I gently pulled the cloth aside. I stepped back as a fluttering ball of feathers flew into my face and past me. I turned in shock as Ai, wings vibrating rapidly, rose and disappeared into the blue sky.

She had been wrong. The bird would escape, fly free. Poor Shuang, she would be heartbroken. But why was the bird loose in the tent? – she always put him back in his cage before she went to sleep.

'Shuang darling – time to get up!' I ducked my head into the tent and there she was, sleeping peacefully. Then I noticed the cage. The door hung open and the tiny wire lock seemed to be broken. It looked as if the wire had been cut by something. So that was why Ai had been free.

'Shuang?' She had not moved, and I was concerned. I went over and touched her cheek. Her eyelids flickered as I spoke again, this time with real concern. 'Shuang, what is wrong? Are you ill?'

I slipped my hand under her head and lifted her as her eyes opened. She stared ahead. I reached for the cup containing rainwater which stood by the birdcage.

Her lips opened slightly, the lower lip drooping, her tongue lolling. I tipped water into her mouth and she coughed. He body shook, her limbs twitched violently and her eyes rolled upwards; strange grunts came from her throat. Was it some kind of fever? I had to fetch the doctor! I gently lowered her head back onto the pillow as her eyes focused once on mine, then became unseeing.

I became aware there was blood on my hand.

Then I noticed the tiny pencils of sunlight streaming down. Looking up, I saw perforations in the canvas roof. I looked at Shuang more closely. Just above her hairline was a circular mark. The skin was ringed with black, shrivelled back so I could see white bone beneath, and a hole, a hole neatly drilled through the bone. Her body shook with spasms once more, and then she lay still.

I knew what it was. That pattering – shooting stars! Tiny

meteorites! Of all the impossible things to happen. And I had said she was lucky. No, I was wrong and she was right: she was unlucky. And she had been right about the other things: Heaven had indeed called her and Ai had not left her while she still truly lived.

Elinor

Published in the magazine 'The Horror Express' (by Posy).

Flying, with her dark hair streaming,
Elinor, her pale face gleaming,
In the moonlight plummets down,
To lie broken on the ground.

Morning comes and lifeless eyes,
Open to the brightening skies.
Hidden in the brush and bramble,
Elinor's body in the tangle.

The soul has fled her blackened flesh,
Each day winds its fearful mesh.
Through the body, in decay,
Fresh corruption makes its way.

At night, the body moves, then stands,
Rising up with outstretched hands,
Tattered flesh and broken bone
Gently seeking their way home.

In the castle, dark and dour,
Elinor's body mounts the tower
To the room where Ranulf's sleeping,
Where before, that maid lay weeping.

contd ...

Through the castle, strong men hear
Fearsome music, fell and weir.
From Sir Ranulf's tower comes screaming –
Desperate! Frantic! – are they dreaming?

Ranulf lies in foul, black foment,
Body wracked in deadly torment,
Stricken face with bulging eyes,
Horror paints his sad demise.

While below the tower's height,
Wonderful in that dark night,
Lustrous silver flowers bloom,
Marking now Elinor's tomb.

T'nah

What's in a name?

'Please sit down,' I said to the young, fair-haired girl.

'Thank you.' She had a pleasant, soft voice. I took to her at once.

As she settled, I busied myself with the tools of my trade. The job description, her CV and the summary evaluation card were laid out in front of me. I checked the details.

'Right, Miss Johnson. Welcome to R and M Products.' I smiled. 'My name is Mrs Wetherby and I'm going to have an informal chat with you prior to a possible formal interview.'

'So you'll decide if I go forward?'

'No, Miss Johnson, I will make a standardised report for the selectors. Part of this is a basic personality test. You see, here at RMP we try to balance personality types in the workplace and suit them to jobs which will satisfy them – and encourage productivity of course.' I gave a small laugh. She smiled.

'So, if by any chance you are not called for a formal interview, in all likelihood it will be about quotas and not any deficiency on your part, you understand.'

She nodded.

'Right, Miss Johnson, let us begin.'

'You can call me by my first name.' She grinned.

I ticked another box on the card. Good social skills – what a pleasant young lady!

'Thankyou, we approve of a less formal atmosphere

here.' I consulted the record form with her CV.

'Well Tina, what makes you want to work here?'

'T'nah,' she said.

'I beg your pardon?'

'My name – it's T'nah.' Her expression was not so pleasant now, almost aggressive.

I consulted the sheet again. 'T-I-N-A?'

She nodded.

'Tina?' I tried saying it a bit differently, but to me 'Tina' was 'Tina'.

This time she did look annoyed. She spoke slowly as if I was retarded. 'It is spelt T-I-N-A, but it is pronounced T'nah. Surely that's obvious?'

I tried again and eventually I got close enough for her to nod approval.

'So, T'nah, I'm glad we sorted that out. Sorry I was a rather slow.'

'Oh, you weren't so bad. I'm always amazed how stupid people are, though. Some of them don't even get it right when I explain, keep calling me Tina. Tina indeed – how dumb can some people get?'

'That must be most annoying, er, T'nah.'

'It's disrespectful. Most people can't even bother. They just read it off a sheet or something and make stupid assumptions. I get really mad sometimes.'

'I'll bet you do.'

I marked her card.

We continued the interview. She did quite well in some areas.

I rounded off with the final question. She thought for a minute, then replied, a pleasant smile on her face.

'Well, what I would bring to the company is a sensitive understanding of people tempered by patience and tolerance.'

What a good answer! I shook her hand, gave her the usual information about when she would hear from us, and showed her out.

As I tidied up the documentation and wrote my short additional comments on the card, Jane poked her head round the door.

'She any good?'

'I don't think so, not for a customer service position, Jane.'

'Oh, shame. Better luck with the next one then, eh, Tina?'

'Indeed,' I said, and smiled.

Modern Times

Best sung to the tune of 'Bonnie Dundee'.

Bobby and Norah were lost in the fog,
There was no sign of old Panzer, their dog.
Bobby had thought he was there at their side,
But Panzer had run back to Mrs McBride.

As the fog thickened, young Bobby was foxed.
Norah got frightened and pulled up her socks.
She clutched at Bob's arm with a hell of a grip,
Bob stiffened his back and she bit on her lip.

The fog was a mantle that covered the ground,
The hollows and hummocks, the heather all round.
It's going to be dark soon, young Norah opined,
Looking at Bobby and reading his mind.

Suddenly there was a bark from the left.
Panzer was scrambling up out of a cleft.
As he approached them Bob saw with delight
Something he held in his mouth, very tight.

At home they had biscuits and cake with their tea.
Mrs McBride sat and chortled with glee.
Bobby and Norah gave thanks that she'd let
Panzer bring out Bobby's GPS set.

Buena Vista

I tried a flavour of US small town atmosphere with this. Some US friends have said it's okay.

They called it 'Buena Vista'. And so it was – until Old Man Atkins arrived in town. We started seein' his big white limo around. First time, it passed along Main Street where Ben and I were sat on a bench, enjoying the spring air.

'Whoo-eee, that's some motor!' Ben sat up and grinned in admiration.

'Jes' one of those rich city folks, I guess. Where's he headin'?'

Ben got up and walked across to the corner, so he could see which way the limo turned. 'BV, looks like,' he called. Now what could be goin' on out there? I wondered. I soon found out.

'Damn great factory!' Charlie Wilson was all fired up. His redder-than-usual face stared at me.

'And what d'you expect me to do, Charlie?'

'Why, stop him! Stop him, of course.'

'Ain't no law against buildin' factories, Charlie. Providin' he got the permits an' all.'

'You better check all that then, Gabe.'

'I ain't no lawyer, Charlie.'

'No, but it's part of your job, and nobody else can do it.'

Well, he was wrong on his first statement, but right on the second. Besides which, I was very fond of Buena Vista myself. Me and Beth did our courtin' there, longer ago than I care to remember and I kinda had a soft spot for the place. Buena Vista is, I suppose, best described as meadows. The river wanders through lush green grass and trees. At the edges are small hillocks and clefts which run up into the sides of the hills that surround the river valley for a short stretch, which are covered in a forest of bushes and scrubby trees. You can walk to it from the edge of town and it has always been regarded as common land. People graze horses, go for walks on Sunday, and of course the kids and young folk play and stroll there of an evening. It's a kind of heritage. The town wouldn't be the same without it. Most folks call it 'BV'.

Charlie Wilson's house was one of four or five close to the meadows, sited on a rise where the valley sides flattened out. The original ranch here had been called Buena Vista, and Charlie and the others had built houses on its remains. There were rumors, though. Not bad, but a bit weird. Some said the ranch owner built a mill on the river, and it burned down, taking the ranch with it. This was long before my time, or my pop's. Grandpa used to mutter about it when he was alive, but of course at that age, I wasn't one for listenin' to ramblin' old folks. Times I wished I had, though. There were still parts of the ranch left – the stone chimneys and walls were now incorporated into the houses. But there was nothing left to hint that there had ever been anything on the Buena Vista meadows.

I checked everything. Atkins was taking advantage of Government policy. They needed processing plants to support hog-farmers, and Atkins had got special clearance at State level. I told Charlie, I'm not sure he listened too hard.

One day, Old Man Atkins turned up. Ben yelled to me as the big limo pulled up outside the office, and it wasn't long before the man himself stomped in through the door, which was opened by a uniformed chauffeur – we don't see many of them in Cranesville.

'You the Sheriff?' He rested one hand on a silver-topped walking cane, and poked a big fat cigar at me with the other. He was a scrawny feller, sort of weasely – wouldn't look you straight in the eye, know what I mean?

'Sure am, Mister …?'

'Atkins. Call me "Boss".'

'Well, er, Mister Atkins, what can I do for you? Wont'cha take a seat?' He looked uncomfortable, wobbling slightly on his stick.

'No! I want you to come with me. I demand police protection!' Turned out he'd been out to BV and old Charlie Wilson had had words.

'Old Charlie won't do you no harm, Mr Atkins, he's just as tame as a pussycat. Loud, I grant you, but there's no harm in him.'

'All the same, I'd rather be safe. I'm not in good health. Besides which, it's my right. I pay taxes – plenty of 'em.' I'll bet he did, what with that fancy motor and all.

'Okay, okay.' I decided I'd better keep an eye on this anyhow. I followed him up to BV in the patrol car with Ben. There was another car as well – a couple of sharp guys in suits, city types.

Sure enough, when we got to BV, there was Charlie, pacin' up and down. He had the hounds out. Now that wasn't nice. City folks don't understand dogs. Those hounds wouldn't hurt a person, but they made so much noise growlin' and whinin', you wouldn't want to test out whether they would or wouldn't.

'Now Charlie, tie up them hounds, will ya?' He eventually obeyed, and the party got out of their cars. The chauffeur helped Atkins out, then a white-uniformed nurse followed. Well, I'll tell you, our jaws must've dropped to the ground! It musta bin' purely comical to watch, but of course none of the city types was interested in us.

'Put your tongue away,' I told Ben, who was fixin' his gaze on that nurse like a hound on point.

'But ...'

I knew what he meant. We'd never seen anything like her in Cranesville, 'cept on the movies that is. Sure, we'd had our share of pretty girls, my Beth for one. But this girl sorta *shone* – she was glossy, sleek, I can't describe it. Ben was moonstruck.

Anyways, I made sure the old man could get about his business without Charlie annoyin' him too much. After a while, with a black look at me, Charlie stomped off up to his house, takin' the hounds.

I kept an ear on what the slick guys were sayin'. One was a sort of architect – he had lots of drawings and plans. The other was in construction – I never before saw a builder in a city suit, but that's what he was alright. Well, these guys scrambled around, poking sticks in the ground and lookin' about with squinty eyes, until they eventually came back to Old Man Atkins in the limo. I looked round for Ben. He was settin' over on a rock with that nurse. She was gigglin' and tossin' those golden curls around, flutterin' her eyes at him. That boy is sure headin' for a big disappointment, I thought. I sidled up to the limo. Seemed like everythin' was fine, accordin' to the two guys. They could build whatever they were goin' to build 'on time and on budget' as they said. After a while of this, Old Man Atkins started chucklin' fit to bust. Then he caught sight of me.

'See Sheriff, the wisdom of our benevolent government?' I didn't know what he was talkin' about, but he kept on talkin'. 'Not only do they guarantee me prices to process the hogs, but they give me an enormous sum of money to build the factory in the first place. Very generous, huh?' I gathered the old man was being sarcastic. 'And do you know what the best thing about it is, Sheriff? The very best thing?'

'No sir, I don't.' I tipped my hat back on my head and wiped my brow.

'They pay me …' He broke off, coughing, looking around for the nurse, who soon came running and gave him something to calm him.

'They even pay me …' he continued eventually,'… for every asshole. Every goddam hog asshole I produce.'

'What the hell d'you do with a hog's asshole?'

Old Man Atkins beamed – a wide grin split his face. 'I don't know, and I don't care. I just know they pay me for every goddam hog's asshole.' He started coughing again, and the nurse settled him, ready to leave. I saw her cast a look at Ben, which had me wondering. Then they packed up.

I told Charlie. It was only fair. 'It's a hog-processing plant. They render down the fat, everything.'

'But it'll stink like hell.' The wind usually blew out of the town up the river and over BV to the houses. They'd get all of it, most of the time. 'And the river!' he exclaimed. Sure enough, they planned to use the water, so it might be pretty messy as it flowed past the town. He shook his head. 'How do they get stuff in and out?'

'Trucks from Brownston,' I told him. Charlie looked up along the blacktop that ran past his house. 'And they're talking about running a link to the railhead other side of town.'

He gazed for a while down the valley, which lay peaceful and green in the afternoon sun. Then he said one word: 'No', then strode off. I hoped he wasn't thinking of any foolishness.

Ben was looking dreamy.

'Ben!' I said sharply.

We got back in the car.

You see, Charlie wasn't always called 'Wilson'. His family took that name so as to fit in better after the ranch burned down, so I heard tell. See, some people said his great-grandpa had a hand in it. No – not like that, I don't mean he set a fire or nothin'. But he was, well, I don't know what you'd call it these days, a shaman? A witch-man?

It was said that BV had been a sacred place, long before the white men came. The story went that the ranch owner had been warned many times, but went ahead and built the mill right on the very spot. Charlie's great-grandpa had been up in the hills the night of the fire – well away from the area. But some had heard drumming and chanting, and you know how rumors get about.

They started excavating. Well, right from the beginnin' things started to go wrong. They lost a machine. Yup! Lost it. It plunged down a deep hole, come from somewhere. Lucky the driver jumped off as it tilted slowly, and splashed ashore as the giant yellow thing sank into the river and the boggy ground. Well, what a fuss! They had testers testing the ground, the Union pulled the digger drivers out. They lost weeks before it was all fixed.

Then came the freak storm. They'd brought in some temporary buildings. Neat little boxes all stacked up and dotted around. One night, there was a hell of a storm. Didn't touch the town, but sure as hell wrecked the camp at BV. I was called up there. What a sight! The neat little cabins were all tumbled over and thrown around, like a child's wooden blocks. Luckily no-one had been moved into them, so nobody was hurt. But the labor refused to countenance goin' up there to stay after that. There was little spare room in town – and truth be told, little welcome for any men working on the project, so they had to bring them in from Brownston every day.

Charlie had been quiet for some time – I hadn't seen hide nor hair of him. I knew he had a place up in the hills, so he was probably up there, sulking. It was funny, that place of his. I had tried to find it once, when his pa was bad. I hunted everywhere. I had heard sounds – the dogs, wood being split, but never found the cabin. I'd turn a corner, expectin' fully to see it there, and it was just another wall of rock. Eventually I'd hollered for Charlie, and he'd stepped up behind me – gave me a hell of a shock. I was too occupied givin' him the news to wonder where he'd come from at the time, but it's bothered me since.

Old Man Atkins was hoppin' mad!

'It's sabotage!' he yelled. 'Someone's deliberately causin' these problems.'

'Mr Atkins, that's pure fancy. You've had holes in the ground, storms, and now this. How could any person have done it?'

'I don't know, Sheriff, but it ain't natural.'

He did have a point. An awful lot of things had gone wrong, and this latest thing, well …

'It's that Charlie what's-his-name!'

'Now, now,' I scolded, 'you can't go accusin' innocent folks no matter how important you are. Do you have any proof? Have you seen Charlie around?'

He shook his head. Then he said something funny. 'I see his face.'

'Wha'?'

'I see his face in my dreams. He's sort of all painted-up with feathers an' all. He's shouting at me.'

I laughed. 'Sounds mighty like conscience.'

He got up, red-faced. His chauffeur helped him up – the nurse was outside with Ben again. 'You are damned impertinent, sir!' He was shaking with rage. He was probably right. It wasn't my place to judge him, so I apologized. This placated him, but he left anyway.

I called Ben. 'Come on, let's go see what's happened.'

Ben and I looked down on the site. 'Sure looks strange,' I said.

'Just crazy.' Ben shook his head.

They'd brought in a big crane, one of those tall, skinny things held up by wires. It was bent right over about halfway, the top sort of knocked over one side. This was too much. I'd have to talk to Charlie.

'Charlie! Charlie! I know you're here. This is important, come out.' I could hear him. Well, I had heard him as I approached. Chanting. I could hear the hounds, too.

'What is it, Gabe?' Once again, he appeared from nowhere.

'We gotta talk, Charlie. This is not the way.'

'I am not letting that place get built.'

'Listen, Charlie. I talked to Old Man Atkins. Sure, the project is set back. But he's insured, and he's damn stubborn. He is not going to give up. Eventually, someone's gonna get hurt, you know that.'

'I am very careful.'

'I know, Charlie, but believe me, this is dangerous.'

'You want me to stop, to let Changuanma be despoiled.'

I had never heard it called that. 'I don't want that, Charlie, I want you to do it different – be a little cleverer.' I pulled out a copy of the Wall Street Journal I'd picked up in Brownston. Charlie looked surprised. 'Let's go sit on your porch and talk this through.'

I didn't see where it changed, but suddenly we were in a clearing, with trees and a pool fed by a spring. On one side was a cabin, and in the center of the clearing a tepee, a grand, ceremonial one. It looked real old, but the colors were as fresh as if they'd just been painted. On the ground near a fire lay a tumble of wooden blocks and a long, bent piece of wire. Someone had dug a small deep hole in the earth alongside. 'Oh, Charlie,' I chided, and shook my head. He had the grace to look ashamed. We sat. I opened up the newspaper and explained my idea.

'You won't be having any more problems, Mr Atkins. I'm keeping an eye on things now.'

He looked surprised. 'I thought you …'

'I uphold the law, Mr Atkins. I have to be impartial.'

'Well, good, good.' A smile almost passed across his face. 'There'll be something in this for you. I always repay favors.'

'No thanks, Mr Atkins, no favors, just doin' my job.' I tipped my hat. He was gazing over the site. The foundations had gone in and they were starting on the frame, clanging and welding the beams together. 'They still goin' to pay you for every hog's asshole, Mr Atkins?'

A frown crossed his face. He looked a little harassed. 'What? Oh yes, oh yes … probably.'

'Yup!' I thought, turning to leave, the plan must be working. He wasn't so cocksure now.

The last time anyone saw Old Man Atkins was in Main Street. Charlie had been good as gold, and our plan was working. But he just could not resist taking one last swipe at the Old Man. Guess I couldn't blame him. This big refrigerated truck pulled up, right in Main Street. The driver jumped out, looking really spooked. A crowd of us hurried out. The school kids were coming back from a ball game, so pretty much half the town was there.

'What's wrong?' I asked, stepping forward. The driver was hanging round the back of the truck, agitated.

'There's someone in there. Banging on the side.'

'What's in there?'

'Hogs' assholes.'

The schoolteacher tried to shoo the kids away, but this was just too good to miss.

Old Ma Pride cackled, 'Sounds like one of the assholes wants out.' The whole crowd chuckled. Once we'd opened up, they chuckled even more, calling and hooting. A hill of neatly-packed hogs' assholes had fallen out of the back of the truck. In the midst of it sat Old Man Atkins, shivering, coughing and looking completely bewildered.

'Oh, he was right.' Ma Pride couldn't leave it alone. 'It *is* full of assholes!'

We got the old man cleaned up and settled and called up his chauffeur, who had been waiting for him up at the factory. 'How did I get in there?' he kept repeating.

That was the last we saw of Old Man Atkins. The nurse came to work for the Doc when Atkins went broke. Can't figure why a girl like that would do that, but Ben's pretty pleased.

They sold off the factory to a company who dismantled it and shipped it off to Kansas. The roads and the foundations are crumbling nicely, already sinking. You won't know anything has been there by next spring. Of course, Charlie's helping.

Charlie! I had a word with him about Atkins, and you know what he said?

'I had to have a bit of fun, Gabe, all that tinkering with share prices to spook his investors – just too damn boring.'

'But I was right, Charlie.'

'You were right, Gabe.'

We'd seen our last asshole.

In Smoke

One of Posy's first poems

In smoke,
My dearest lover sings
Our life, his hopes, my fears.

He rises,
Leaving me below,
Alone and dress'd in tears.

Clasped in my hands
His last bequest,
The charm that I have worn,
From that first inkling of distress
Until this deathly morn.

I hold it now in anger dark,
Oppressed by what has been

For he is taken, borne aloft,
This day in Skibbereen.

Regret

I think now of the days
That sped unheeded past your startled eyes,
Unreeling time
You did not have.

My only hope is
That your winter thoughts
Allowed some room
For summer.

And when you left me,
You held fresh flowers in your gaze
And supped sweet-scented air
Besides.

The End of the Line

This story uses a similar voice to 'A Hole in the Wall of the Universe ...' and has some connections with 'Minna'. Much of the description is true: I have been to Khabarovsk and I too, have strolled by the Amur River.

The small village of Petrovsk, where I grew up, does not have a graveyard. When my mother died ten years ago, we had to put her body on the rail truck to take her to town. But part-way, the engine stalled. We pushed until night, my daughter Galya, her husband Dmitry and I. But it was nearly autumn and snow began to fall. We knew we had to walk back to my mother's house. As the ground was not yet frozen we buried my mother by the track – we could not leave her exposed. My Galya cried: 'Mother, what is to become of us?' I told her good times were coming, they had promised.

My father died in a mining accident when I was a young girl. No road had ever been built to the village and when the mine there closed thirty years ago and the trains stopped coming, the company gave us the motorised rail truck to get to Yekaterin. The women used to sit in it with their produce on market days, and wave as they went off down the track. As time passed, breakdowns became more frequent.

The big trains shake our apartment in Yekaterin and the empty wagons clank over the joint in the rail as they snake through the outskirts. Later, they will return filled with ore, quieter, but with a deep, rumbling weight.

As a child in Petrovsk, I used to love riding the big, slab-faced engines into town. I knew all the drivers, called them 'uncle'. They were cheerful, smiling. Sometimes my mother would offer some of the vegetables she carried. They always refused, telling us to save them for the market.

When things changed fifteen years ago, the news was good. We would be rich, they said. The pigs in the Capital would no longer rob us of the money we never saw, they said. The Mayor, Aleksei, a close ally of the Regional Governor, assured us the good times were on their way. They seemed to be, for him. Gone was the Lada – he acquired a shiny, black-windowed Japanese car. He swaggered around with his hangers-on. When the pensions stopped, we had to help the old people. I called him by his boyhood name – 'Alyosha. Alyosha, where are these good times? Where is the money?' – He was sorrowful, he apologised. It was not his fault, he explained. 'Would your Alyosha not tell you the truth?' he asked me. So I waited.

Dmitry is no good for my Galya. At first she would speak about him, 'My Dima likes this … My Dima is going to do that …' She was full of him. And he was polite: 'My dear mother-in-law,' he would call me. He worked in the shipping office, booking in the trains and calculating the loads. He seemed bright, with a future. But then the trains began to diminish and he lost his job. He will not try to find another, he has no ambition. He has a pension, he says. But it is not enough. The only manager they kept at the office was Aleksei's cousin, a man who is drunk all day. And he too acquired a Japanese car.

When we were first married, my Kostya took me to the city of Khabarovsk for our honeymoon. We stayed with his cousin. It was an enormous city; I have never seen a place so big. We went on the railway, first in the cab of one of the ore trains to the main line, then on a long, long passenger train. Kostya's sister, Svyeta, was a supervisor on the train. She showed us the fine compartments, the beds where the passengers slept. On the way, we were not allowed to use the compartments. The Chief Supervisor would not agree: 'Svyetlana, you know it is not allowed.' Kostya was upset. He told me he was sorry he did not have enough money for us to travel properly, but I said that was not important. Coming back, we were luckier, the Chief was Svyeta's friend, and we passed a night in supreme comfort, sharing with two nice students returning to university at Alma Ata who were clever and polite. In the morning Svyeta brought us tea and some bread. We stopped at stations where we could buy food, but Kostya had little money, so we had black bread with our tea.

In Khabarovsk, we had a lovely time. I still dream of it. In the fine weather, we strolled by the Amur River. They had a special pavement for people to walk. It was hard to believe that anyone would build a place just to stroll in gardens with flowers by the water. I had never seen so much water before, flowing so swiftly. Richly-dressed people passed by and small children played. They sold ice-cream, ice-cream such as I had never tasted. And when Kostya's cousin, Slava, pointed up the river and said, 'There is China!' I shuddered. We were so close to our enemies.

In the markets, food was plentiful. We ate well, taking food home to repay Slava and his wife for their hospitality. They seemed amused. On Sunday, we helped Slava's wife's father collect potatoes. We had such fun! We took a boat across the river to an island. I had never been on the water. The deck was flat and we all stood huddled together as it moved up and down beneath us in a most peculiar way. We went with Ivan to his allotment, such hard work! But no harder than back home – and more fun. People were laughing, calling out to each other. Occasionally, someone would start a song. At lunchtime we sat eating bread, and they made tea. There were families, even small children helping. Going back, we each had a backpack and two bags, all full of potatoes. As the sun set, we bade farewell to each other and made our separate ways, spreading out up the hills back through the town and out to the houses on the outskirts. Ivan gave us a fine meal, with some vodka. As we returned to Slava's flat, we were all very merry. I looked out at the vast river, to the mountains beyond, and thought, over there is a different country. It was hard to believe where I was.

I was sorry to get off that long train on the way back. I had never seen life like I did then. I wished I was like Svyeta, seeing the cities, the places in our great land. But as we huddled, waiting for the next clanking ore train which would take the branch line, I told Kostya I was happy, that I had never seen such wonderful sights. I thanked him and he seemed happier. Kostya was a good man, he always meant well. He was never rough or angry with me, only with himself. When he raged, when he drank, he was angry with himself. I knew that. I always knew. I told him so, often, as he apologised.

I remember sitting in the cab of the train, watching the lights of our town appear out of the gloomy night. I was pleased to be home. But we never left again. That sounds so final. Certainly, Kostya will never leave again, not now. I place flowers on his stone every Sunday. It is possible I might, but how? I have a small pension and Galya is a good girl, but she has Dmitry, and they have little. Sometimes she does work for Aleksei's company, helping in the train office. Trains still run to Yekaterin and the big mine is still operating, but we have never seen the 'good times' that he promised. These days, Aleksei lives in a grand house outside the town, in a walled estate with several others and guards outside. We don't see him much now, only his 'assistants' who run things. He owns 'Joint Stock Companies' with Americans I am told. They have contracts with the mining company and the Government. It is all private now, and independent. Perhaps that is best for our country.

In the old days, people helped each other. The drivers, the supervisors on the long passenger trains, we worked together. Now it takes money: you must pay the driver, you must pay the supervisor and you must pay one of Aleksei's assistants. If you offer them food or vodka, they laugh. I have tried.

I would love to leave, to visit Khabarovsk again and remember those happy times just once before I die. But I'm sure I never shall.

Mosaic

A poem is a mosaic of words …

Every word a bright, sharp, jewel
Of different shape and hue.
Coloured, blended, large and small,
Placed in mosaic by a careful hand.

Trace the story.
Step along the shining words,
Each one a gem to savour.

Follow threads.
Some bold,
Some crossing, turning, weaving.

Lean closer.
They unwind,
Deceiving.

Then stand back.
The whole scene jumps to view.
A pattern complete.

The Presence of Jalendu

Previously published in 'Cadenza' magazine, this story is about absence and things not said.

The early-morning rush hour crowds would swarm round him, an eddy in the human tide. I saw him as a perturbation in the smoothly-flowing streets, an obstacle to be avoided. Each day he would sit on the hard stone corner, begging. For nearly twenty years I have seen him from my shop. When I opened in the morning, he was there. When I pulled down the shutter each evening, he was there.

I knew his name: Jalendu. Someone told me. I never talked to him myself.

Sometimes I waved and he nodded back. When it was quiet I stared across at him, watching him sitting quietly. He never came to the shop. He hardly ever moved. I don't know what time he arrived in the morning, where he went when he left, or if he left at all. I never crossed the street.

I would ask my brother, when I had been away: how was the shop and how was Jalendu? He would tell me, 'fine' and 'still there'. And so it would be.

I wondered about Jalendu – his age, where he came from. I watched as people passed him, trying to work out how much money he gathered. People did not see him. Even those who gave money – I watched the movement of the arm and hand, dropping coins into his bowl – did not look directly at him. They passed by. I never saw anyone trip or stumble over him, even at the height of the commuter's rush to work or when the tradesmen were hurrying along the street. Even in the rain, to the tangled umbrellas bobbing and swaying above the crowds, he stayed invisible. He would don a large hat and pull a waterproof round him. His eyes seemed simply to gaze ahead. I rarely saw an expression on his face – just his nod.

When my son was small, I used to send him across with something for Jalendu. An apple, some fruit, nuts, a sweet thing. Daya enjoyed it. He was old enough to cross the road, and felt important. And he liked to give. I would ask him what Jalendu said. 'Thank you,' Daya would grin. Jalendu would look across and nod his head.

When Daya was fourteen, he told me he did not wish to give Jalendu any more 'presents' as he called them. He said it was wrong, his mother had told him so. I asked Amara what she had said. She said I was foolish to give away our profits to an old beggar, and that Daya must learn to be businesslike, or we would starve in our old age. 'That boy is our future' she told me.

He certainly took over the hard work, I no longer had to pay my brother or uncle if I decided to take a little time off.

As time went by, I began to stay at home more often. Amara complained, asking why I did not help Daya. 'You can't leave it all to the boy, he has a life to lead,' she scolded. She and her friends were always busy, chattering, filling our house. She said Daya worked so hard and I should help him as much as I could until I had to retire. So I started going to the shop again every day.

We had to visit Amara's brother. His wife had died and we had to go away for the funeral. It was the other side of the country, to the west, a long railway journey.

When I came home, I joined Daya at the shop. For half

the day, all was as usual. Then I realised. Something was missing: Jalendu. 'Where is he?' I asked my son. He looked puzzled. I told him, 'Jalendu, the man who you used to take small gifts to.' He told me he did not know. I waited for weeks, but he was gone. I asked other shopkeepers. They all seemed puzzled. 'Oh, the old beggar?' Eventually they would say, 'I don't know, he's gone.'

Is that all? Is that what is left? I thought.

So, for the first time, I crossed the road. I pushed my way through the rush hour crowds bustling past. I found it difficult. I went to Jalendu's corner, approached the place where he had sat for so long. The pushing and shoving stopped; people flowed round me. I could stand comfortably, raise my arms, sit. So I did.

Sometimes now I cross the road to sit in Jalendu's place. In his sanctum, I watch the crowds pass. I am peaceful and calm. People throw coins at my feet, even though there is no bowl and I am well-dressed. I leave them.

My wife is unhappy. Daya is unhappy. 'Why do you do this, Dad?'

I have no answer.

With Eyes Whose Panes …

They say the eyes are the windows of the soul.

With eyes whose panes obscure a curtained depth
of shadows hid in secret lampless rooms,
I see a growing resonance of death:
the damp, decay, and stillness of the tomb.

The silent, prowling panther of the night
is threading through the sunbeams' golden bars.
My eyes engage the swiftly-fading light
to wrest it from the secret, sullen stars.

In desperation, fearing worse than life,
my resolution strengthens its control.
I sniff the air. But, slicing like a knife,
a deadly calm now enters in my soul.

The Black Boy

I like writing in an old-fashioned style, maybe because I read so many short stories in this style in my youth.

I had been somewhat restless since the death of my wife, and made a decision to use my Army pension to retire to the country. After some searching, I was fortunate enough to find an old rectory, set in gardens next to a wood running down into a small valley, secluded and peaceful but close to a village. It was ideal for my purpose. The building was all one would expect of a country rectory: tall chimneys, steepled roof, and arched windows. Inside it was in excellent condition, with several light and airy bedrooms, a friendly, stone-floored kitchen and best of all, a large study lined with bookcases and wide French windows opening onto the lawn: perfect for the intended task of writing my memoirs.

Gazing round the grounds after the removal men had done, I drank in the tranquillity and resolved I should be happy to spend the rest of my days in such a place, simply writing, and in doing so, trying to forget the fruitless attempts to contact my dead wife through spiritualism. If only I could discover why she had done what she had.

I settled in well. The previous owner had an agreement that in return for rights to hunt in the woods and gather timber, the grounds would be tended regularly and maintained. I also inherited a housekeeper, who visited daily, a woman of the village, one Mrs Arnold, the gardener's wife. I engaged craftsmen for minor repairs and improvements, though in truth, little was needed. A fine summer passed into autumn, heralded by evenings when mist rolled in from the woods and surrounded the garden, cocooning it in a peaceful blanket that swallowed all noise. It was sometimes eerie, the only sound the occasional muffled call of a pigeon in the distance.

About the garden were placed several small stone benches. There was one such in a far corner near the edge of the wood, and on one misty October evening that is where I saw the boy. He sat on the bench: a slight, indistinct figure, but clearly a boy – a boy who would be about the same age as my son Harold, if only … I walked towards him, calling out what I intended to be a greeting. As the mist swirled, I wiped a hand across my eyes and when I resumed my gaze, the bench was empty. I assumed the child had slipped away, mistaking my call for a protest at his trespass. I was driven to ask Mrs Arnold about him.

'A boy?' Her face lost its amiability and she looked thoughtful. 'A boy, Captain Threadgold? We do have some boys in the village, but no one … what did you say … ten?'

'That age I would guess.'

'I don't know any such, sir, certainly none who might come to your garden on a damp evening and sit there.' I felt Mrs Arnold was being less than truthful. This ungentlemanly thought surprised me, but something about her manner told me I was right. I did not press her on the matter.

The next day, she tapped on my study door and entered with my morning tray. As she poured the tea, she spoke hesitantly, softly, 'The boy, sir …' She finished pouring and looked up at me. I asked her to continue. 'Don't go near him, sir, leave him alone. If you see it, turn away.' Her words drove a chill through me. Here in my haven of peace, a seed of uncertainty had been placed, something unpleasant. I was angry when I spoke in return and asked her to explain.

Her grandmother had told her the story. A simple story: a village boy drowned while playing in the wood. I had neither explored the wood nor ventured beyond the lawns and I was puzzled how someone might drown there. It transpired that in the bottom of the valley lay a pond, which at times became deep enough to drown a child. She told me the boy's spirit haunted the wood, and had been occasionally seen by others. 'But he's not nice, sir. Despite what you may think you see, it's not nice, keep away from it, the Black Boy!' Mrs Arnold was in a state of some distress. I could get no more from her, let alone as to why the child was referred to as the 'Black Boy'. I was moved to excuse her for the rest of the morning, and she left gratefully, though with a string of warnings in her wake.

That very evening, I encountered the boy again, still at a distance, but this time clearer, more solid. It had to be a boy. I was sure he was smiling at me. Here was tangible, or near-tangible evidence of a spirit contact. A fleeting thought told me that if indeed this was a drowned village boy, he might be a conduit to my wife and son. Heedless of my housekeeper's warnings, I walked towards him. As I did so, his image wavered, then faded back into the wood, into the mist. I called out. But he was gone.

The next day, I donned some stout wellingtons, thick trousers and jacket, and picking up my walking staff, set out into my wood. Passing by the bench where the boy had sat, I sensed a chill, but shrugging it off, I pressed on and found a narrow gap in the undergrowth opening onto a trail, obviously well-used, possibly by Mr Arnold the gardener. I followed the path, choosing at each branch a downhill direction. Eventually, the slope began to level out and I calculated I was nearing the valley bottom. I soon found the pond. It was not large, but my staff sank into the water for some distance.

It was filthy, a rank stench rose from it and an occasional bubble of gas broke the surface, causing the black scum which filled it to swirl gently. It was a festering mass of leaves, rotting in the water, a mess of corruption. I left hurriedly. There was evil here. It was certainly unpleasant – the stench, the miasma surrounding the filthy pond. I thought of the boy, choking and dying in the mess as it filled his mouth and covered his eyes until he succumbed. I shuddered, wondering what torture the poor devil's final moments had been in that evil place. I felt unaccountably tainted, and went back to the house to take a hot bath, refreshing myself in the soothing warmth. I forgot about the pond, and the boy, and for the rest of the day set to at my memoirs, achieving a satisfactory progress before tea.

As dusk fell, I strolled in the garden, replete with my evening meal, a small brandy in my hand and a cigar to my lips. He was there. This time I spoke softly and did not approach too closely. I wooed him with kind words. I spoke about my wife, as a friend, asking for his help. I cajoled, told him I desired his company, wished to talk to him and listen to his thoughts in whatever form he now occupied. I wanted to make him my friend. He stayed, seeming to look at me and hear my words. In the end it was I who left him, sitting on the bench as darkness fell, with a promise to return.

He was there again the following night. Once more I kept my distance and he gave every indication, as far as I could tell, that he was listening to my words. I told him he now had a friend, that we would talk often and I would stay with him, keep him company. I asked about my wife. But he gave no reply. Whether he was able, I knew not, but I persisted, driven by an increasing fascination with this link to the other side.

Mrs Arnold asked if I was feeling well, enquired about

the progress of my writing. In truth I had neglected it of late, spending my days impatiently waiting for dusk and my meeting with the boy. Again she warned me, 'Don't go near it, sir, turn away.' I'm afraid I was a bit short with her.

That evening, it was different; I had an expectation as the bench at the corner of the garden came into view. He was there, and I knew somehow this time I could approach.

As I drew nearer, I made out the seated figure. I uttered wooing words, calling him to me. For the first time, I saw it clearly. I perceived that it was not a boy – it was a thing of blackness, of slime and raggedness, of filthy horror. Its head rose slowly, I saw two demonic red eyes in a black lump of a face, a leering slash of a slimy drooling mouth and I was transfixed. The creature loped towards me. I tried to turn and run, but I could not. Now it was bounding at me, slavering jaws open. An inane giggle filled my ears as it leapt upon me. Arms clamped round my neck, legs around my trunk, and its face, its filthy face, pressed on mine like an amorous lover's. And the stench, the rotten, stinking smell! The mess of corruption clogged my mouth as the creature pressed itself on me, holding me tighter and rubbing its body against me. The filth filled my nostrils and eyes. I heard a bubbling scream and it was mine. Then I was falling backwards under the wet, sagging weight as I choked and vomited my breath away.

We sit here together now, the boy and I. We two are alone in this misty world, as he was for so many years until I came. I am his friend, his first friend, his only friend. And now we are together. We sit on this bench.

Waiting.

The Black Boy's Plea

I wrote this story shortly after the preceding one, as part of a challenge to other writers to produce an alternative or sequel, a challenge to which I myself responded, thus:

I'm sitting here in the garden with my new friend. He is kind, very kind. I've never had a friend before. When I played in the woods with the other boys, we were friends, but I had no special friend. Now I have. He's a grown up, but he is my friend. He told me so for a long time before he joined me.

After the time at the pond, I sat alone for years in this misty world. There are many others who have passed, like me. I sense them, but they are far off and I cannot go where they are, there is something stopping me. If I try hard, I can speak to them. But they are uninterested; they do not seem to care. And none of them ever comes here, to this bench in this corner of the garden as he has.

The house has changed little over the years. It has substance, like me, although I would never approach it. It looks older, but that's all. For years, as the insubstantial ones moved around, few of them ever saw me, even though I tried to make them. The house has had various occupants, but few children. I can talk to children.

One child saw me. They were a happy family, always laughing, playing in the garden, but he would cry out when I came to sit on the bench after wandering the woods, and the adults would cluster round him. He would point towards me, but they saw nothing. They withdrew from the garden and one day he was taken away. His parents stayed for many years, growing older, but after that day they were always sad, not happy any more. They stayed sad until they passed. First the man, then the woman, years later.

My world is misty, and lonely, so lonely. I cannot travel far from the pond and the wood, I am pulled back. I cannot tell how long I have been coming to this bench.

My friend was able to see me before he passed. He talked to me about his son, and his wife. I sensed his burning need. But they were in my world, not his, and I guess that is what formed the link between us. I became a part of them; he focussed his hopes on me. I searched among the passed and found them: his wife – frightening, a whirl of conflict, unresolved grief, sucking me in; and his son, a boy like me. But a handsome boy, a good boy. Better than me, nicer than me.

I needed a friend. He said he was my friend, he would be happy with me. I drew on his need to give him what he secretly wished, and I did so in a spirit of friendship. Now he sits on this bench. He is not sad – he is happy. With me. I know he is. I am sure he is.

He cannot go any further without my help. He does not realise he can, and I will not tell him. It is better this way. I have a friend. He is happy. I have no choice!

The Look

Posy can be thoughtful

Whenever I tried,
my mother said, 'Never mind,
I'll love you even if you fail.'
I remember her Look.

And when
I won – succeeded,
the Look remained.
I wished she'd said, 'I know you'll do it!'

Down the years,
I measured life by failure,
not success.
The Look stayed with me, mocking my ambition.

I always blamed her,
through my life.
But now I've come to understand,
the Look was in my own eyes, not in hers.

Away Day

Virgin trains plus a double glazing salesman?

The smartly-dressed man stood in the doorway holding a large black case.

'Mr. Anstruther?' His beaming smile filled me with confidence. *I liked* him.

'You've come about the …'

'Away Day, yes.'

I led him to the lounge, where my wife offered him tea. He settled himself in a chair opposite me and once I'd got comfortable, leaned forward slightly. Mary perched on a stool next to me.

'Where did you wish to travel, may I ask?'

Mary looked eagerly at me, her eyes shining.

'We'd thought of Brighton.'

'Excellent choice, if I may say to. There are many facilities for an enjoyable day out at Brighton.'

'And which of our fine products do you wish?'

I felt slightly lost. I glanced round at Mary, who shook her head slightly.

'Just an Away Day … for Mary and me and the kids.'

He gave an understanding smile. 'Let us find out together, then.'

I felt slightly ashamed, but reassured. I could trust him.

He took a pad out of his inside pocket and drew a large folder from the case. Opening it, he looked down at the page, then glanced up at me. I had already told him on the telephone which day we wanted to go. He held out a picture. There was a family with two children sitting on what looked like very comfortable seats in nice, bright surroundings, smiling, obviously enjoying themselves. It looked great. Mary and I exchanged excited glances.

'So, what time would the Anstruther family like to set out?' His friendly gaze swept over us.

'Ten o'clock?' I ventured hesitantly.

His gaze swept the page, and his expression changed. His face fell, he looked at us sorrowfully. What was wrong?

'I can't offer you a product at that time, I'm really sorry. Have you an alternative?'

'Well, nine o'clock then. Is there an off-peak fare?'

He smiled. 'Let's discuss that when we have established your needs and found the product that meets them. That is our objective, to meet your needs.'

After consulting his folder, his expression became even more sorrowful. I knew what he was going to say. I felt sorry for him.

'Well, what times do you have?'

'Our job is to meet your needs. If you ask for ten o'clock, we should be able to satisfy your needs.' He shook his head.

'Well, sometime around nine or ten then, we don't mind.'

'Really? That's generous of you.' He leaned even closer and drew a silver pen from his inside pocket and carefully marked the pad on his knee. 'I will tell you now that I've just marked you down for an extra discount in the light of your generous cooperation.'

I was pleased. I looked at Mary as the man flicked through the pages of the folder. 'Yes,' he said, 'there are packages at five-past, twenty-past, twenty-to and five-to the hour. Would any of those suit you?'

Puzzled, I replied, 'Well, yes, of course, that's only five

minutes later … or earlier. That's no problem.'

'Well, that's very generous of you, Mr Anstruther. Considering our failure to meet your initial request.'

'Think nothing of it. It wouldn't hurt to wait five minutes in any case. We could sit in the waiting room?'

The man hesitated a moment, then closed the folder and exchanged it for another, slightly snazzier one which he took from the case. 'I see,' he said, 'you're talking about our Away Day Club product. I hadn't realised.' He held out a picture. The seats looked the same, but the family was better-looking and more smartly dressed. Their smiles were wider. 'Our Away Day Club product offers an exclusive Greeting Lounge with complementary beverages and snacks. That is a wise choice, sir, if I may say so.'

'How much more does it cost?'

He gave me a look that made me feel ashamed for having asked such a question. In the silence that followed, he consulted the folder, then, carefully marking his pad, said, 'So, what say I confirm a ten-forty departure, which will leave you ample time from your chosen ten o'clock timing to enjoy the facilities of the Lounge. I might add that there is also a selection of travel accessories that would help your journey. If I give you this brochure now, you may plan your purchases in advance, as well as taking advantages of special offers on the day.'

I flipped through the brochure. There were books, blow up pillows, DVD's and players, even laptops. I passed it to Mary, who took it eagerly. I was a little worried about the kid's appetite. 'Perhaps we could have some sandwiches on the train?' I asked.

The man looked intently at me. 'Well, of course. I'm sorry, I'm remarkably slow today.' He chuckled. He replaced the folder and drew out another, even snazzier, with a silver border. He held out another picture. This time the family was ultra fashionable, smiling in a far more cultured, superior way. The seats looked the same.

'Away Day Upper Silver includes all the facilities of Club, plus in-journey refreshment and attendance. This product is a really excellent choice for someone, such as yourself, Mr Anstruther, who cares for his family and wants to give them the treatment they deserve. You are a lucky woman, Mrs Anstruther.'

Mary blushed, and took hold of my hand. I felt good. 'I'll have to get a new outfit – and something for the kids,' she whispered. As if anticipating this, the man handed her another brochure with a smartly-dressed woman on the front.

'Perhaps you would like to peruse these fashion items, Mrs Anstruther. They are all fully recommended by us for travel, and they come with a completely free insurance against any damage of soiling while you are with us.' He smiled.

'So,' he said, 'and coming back …?'

'About eight? Could we have a meal on the way back? It would save Mary cooking when we get home.' Mary gave me a grateful glance.

'What a thoughtful man you are, Mr Anstruther. There's not many men who would be so considerate.' He leaned over to his case again.

This time the folder had a gold border. The picture showed the elegant family dining by candlelight, with wineglasses and silver cutlery.

'Away Day Upper Gold is our premier product in this class. You have made a fine choice. Before your return journey, we will serve you aperitifs, some canapés and an amuse-bouche prior to boarding your transport at eight-forty. And with this package, if you wished to stay a little longer, you can defer your return for only a modest extra fee, payable on the day. You will also have the chance to purchase souvenirs in our lounge, so you won't need to carry any gifts around with you during the day.

How thoughtful that was! I hated ending up carrying plastic bags full of things that Mary picked up in the gift shops.

'So, thank you for your time and understanding.' He took out a small calculator and started tapping on it and marking the pad with his pen.

I began to become concerned. How much was all this going to cost?

Eventually, he held out his pad to me with a figure scribbled on it. He was smiling at Mary and holding it so only I could see it.

I gasped. 'That's far too much. I can't afford that!'

Mary pulled her hand away.

The man's face fell. I could tell he was disappointed in me.

'Have you got a digital camera?'

I was surprised, what did he mean?

'Er, no. We had an old one, but it's not very good.'

The man smiled. 'Then I have some excellent news for you. As part of this package, you will receive, free gratis and for nothing, a brand new state-of-the-art digital camera.' He sat back triumphantly, then spoke again. ' Which means that on this trip of a lifetime, you will be able to record all your family's happy moments to look back on and treasure forever. That must be priceless.'

'However,' his face took on a stern look, 'if you really insist that you do not wish to take up this affordable offer, which includes by the way, a finance package which involves minimal monthly payments, we can go back to the basic package, if you insist.'

I felt really bad, and felt mean. Mary tugged at my sleeve. I shook my head. 'No, I'd like the last package, but it's just … rather a lot of money.' I looked up at him appealingly.

The man studied me for a while. Then his face broke into a smile. He raised a finger in the air and exclaimed, 'I have an idea! I apologise for not thinking of it earlier.' He leaned forward again, staring into my face. 'I may have excellent news, something which will enable even you to afford this already highly-affordable package.' Then he drew back. 'If you will allow me to phone my manager, maybe I can solve our little problem …' He waited. I could not believe this man had a manager. What a character he must be!

After the call, he came back and sat down, face expressionless. I had heard snatches of conversation which I didn't fully understand. Suddenly, his face changed. If he had smiled before, now he beamed!

'Let me explain …our caterers have made a generous offer as a loyalty gesture. For selected customers, whom I recommend, they will provide all the additional refreshment and meals, including wine, for free.'

'Does that mean it won't be as good?'

He looked at me with pity. 'No, sir, you will receive the same high-quality service we always offer. It's just a gesture of thanks from our caterers for the opportunities we give them to do such a wonderful job.'

'And …'

He held out the pad again. The figure was still high. 'We have reduced the additional payments included in the Upper Gold package by fifty per cent.' He emphasised the last words triumphantly. Mary clasped my arm. I turned and she was staring at the man with a smile in her eyes.

'But I'm afraid this offer is only open if you decide now. A pretty clear choice, I'd say.' I would swear he looked smug as he smiled at Mary.

I could hardly refuse. I nodded, signed the finance agreements, and it was done. Mary was excited, being very nice to me, cooking a special meal, and sitting down later that evening to pore over the brochures the man had left.

We did enjoy it. The whole trip was memorable, the food tremendous. We were waited on hand and foot, the kids were entertained, the sun shone and Brighton was smashing.

The only false note was while we were waiting for our train. We were sitting in the nice, modern lounge with our tea and biscuits. Mary had her new outfit on, looking really smart. I was playing with the new camera I'd been given, when a train slid into the station. What a train! It was gigantic, powerful, with gold adornments. Through the tinted windows, the interior looked palatial: chandeliers, long leather sofas. Mary and I rose, and called to the children.

'It's early,' Mary said.

'Well, that's good.'

'Excuse me,' a waitress said, barring our way. 'This is not your train.'

From further down the platform, a group of people emerged. They were richly dressed. Behind them a group of tail-coated waiters followed with silver trays, bearing their unfinished drinks and half-empty bottles of champagne. They were ushered onto the train. I noticed several had shiny new cameras, but whereas mine was some nondescript brand, theirs bore the names Canon, Nikon etc. The waiters scurried off and back down the platform as the doors snicked shut and the train slid swiftly out of the station.

'I thought we had the best package,' Mary said. I detected

disappointment in her voice.

'What is that?' I asked the waitress, pointing out at the train.

'Oh, that's the First Class package, sir.'

I remembered seeing another, more imposing folder in the salesman's case. He hadn't even shown it to me.

You are the Grit within my Shell

A kind critic once read an early story of mine and 'talked me down' to a much shorter version (about one quarter length), shedding some of the side-plots, then came back and said 'do you need this other character at all?' This is for him.

I'm finished – It's perfect! I've checked it all through.
I'm pasting it here now to e-mail to you.
I wait with excitement. You're going to say:
'It's perfect!' But no, I read this with dismay:-

The plot doesn't add up, the character's flawed,
That word wasn't used then. I got slightly bored.
Could you make it shorter? Then lengthen the end.
Why not change his sex, or just give him a friend?

His motives are suspect. A man of his age
Wouldn't have done that – It leaps off the page!
Take out a few players; you don't need them all,
And in the third verse you say 'rise' – Why not 'fall'?

What is the true mood of the man in the punt?
Is he really jealous? Or is it a front?
And it's not convincing a woman that size
Could squeeze through a window in such a disguise.

contd ...

You bastard! I'm doubting the worth of your case,
But if you insist, I'll respond with good grace.
Then behind this mask I will weave clever schemes
To defend and reject this attack on my dreams.

I'll explain the impossible, twisting the plot
And introduce mystery, likely as not.
I'll pull any trick that I possibly can
To try to retain my original plan.

By God, I won't change an iota for you!
I'll work and I'll strive just to force it all through.
Triumphant, I've finished, I don't quite know how.
Then back comes your e-mail: *That's much better now!*

The Talent of Julia Cramphorne

A Victorian Tale of Lust and Love

Part 1: In which Mrs Julia Cramphorne is introduced.

I was taking dinner at the club with Old Danbury. I have always thought him a decent fellow, and I enjoy our rather sporadic meetings as he is not only good company, but what's more, he always has an interesting tale to tell. We'd chatted our way through dinner, catching up on the year or so that had passed since we'd last met. John Danbury and I had been in the Guards together – seen a few sights, by gosh! These days I was in the wine trade, and he … Well, I was never sure what he did.

'… bit of this and that,' he would say, stroking his moustache, brown eyes gleaming mischievously. Certainly, he'd financed some trading deals in the Far East and made a packet. That much I knew.

The port sat before us, dark crimson in the cut-glass decanter with glints of reflected firelight. In the club lounge, my fellow members sat, scattered around low tables in fat, brown, quilted leather armchairs.

'So, Danbury.' I raised my glass. 'How are things?' It was the closest I could get to asking the fellow directly what he was doing at the moment. He gave me a curious look, then grinned. His eyes roamed the oak-panelled room, and he drew on his cigar before replying.

'Tonight, Chambers old chap, I'm going to tell you about the most pleasurable experience a man can know.' He sat back in his chair, regarding me with a steely eye, waiting. I struggled to guess what he could mean. Pleasure? He could mean food, but we'd just eaten. He could mean some artistic experience, but I knew he wasn't a chap who appreciated that stuff – tone deaf and ignorant of art. It could only be some kind of physical, sensual experience, and I didn't want to delve too deep into those things, not now. We had shared some wild adventures with local girls in our travels, John Danbury and I, but since marrying Edwina, that side of my nature had calmed. And, respecting Edwina's distaste for such things, I too had forgone the baser side of my nature. Danbury was not married, as far as I knew. My interest was piqued despite myself. I glanced at Danbury again. He maintained his steely gaze, with a hint of amusement now in his polite smile. My mouth opened. And closed.

In the hush of the high-ceilinged room, with muffled conversations buzzing on either side, he spoke in a low voice, leaning towards me, 'Chambers, I can guess what you are thinking, and you are surely on the right track. This is a delicate matter, and not one I would willingly speak about were it not for its importance and unusual nature. There is something I wish to impart, which will doubtless excite your interest and it may be, in time, you too will benefit from the great treasure that is Julia Cramphorne.' He spoke the name with reverence. So it *was* a woman! But what a peculiar way to refer to her: a 'great treasure' – what did he mean? He continued, seemingly oblivious to the puzzlement which must have shown on my face.

'I first became acquainted with Mrs Cramphorne five years ago. From the start I found her a pleasant and amiable companion. We were both staying in Brighton, at the Grand. She was alone, as was I.' He paused a moment, as if in recollection.

'I say!'

His face bore an expression I could not define. 'We became friends …' He looked away for a moment, face serious, staring at nothing. Then his gaze swung back. '… for such a short while.' His face became passive, and his eyes lowered.

'But you have seen her again more recently?' I asked.

Apparently ignoring my question, he continued, 'She is dark, some would say pretty, and at the time she was in her early thirties. She told me her husband had been killed in India, that she had had a child out there, that there had been certain difficulties with the birth, and the girl had not survived. During her recuperation – and this may indeed be a key to what I am about to tell you – she was attended by a local doctor.' I registered surprise, and he held up one hand. 'Yes, it was hardly the done thing, but one of her servants who was especially attached to the lady insisted that the man was brought in secretly. It seems that he had not only medical skills but some mystical art as well.' Danbury sipped his port, and then leaned back.

'I imagine that it was only because she was in such a poor state that she allowed the man near her at all. I gather – because of course the lady was far more delicate in her description than I will be – that the baby had done some damage to her, er, organs of reproduction.' Danbury hesitated, and I felt embarrassed.

'I say, old chap, is this really …'

'Of course!' Danbury's voice rose. 'It's the nub of the whole matter.'

He recovered himself with an apologetic nod. The waiter approached. 'Is everything alright, sir?'

Danbury nodded. 'Yes, yes, very satisfactory. Bring us the brandy, will you, there's a good chap.'

The waiter hurried off. We sat in silence until he returned

and placed the tray with the warm glasses and bottle before us and cleared away the port. I looked at Danbury over the rim of my glass as we exchanged toasts.

'Please continue …' I ventured.

'Yes, where was I?'

'The local doctor …'

'Oh yes.' Danbury took a sip of his brandy and placed the glass firmly down on the table, regarding me directly. 'What I am about to tell you is surprising and may be distasteful. I beg you to accept my assurance that you will at least find this interesting and potentially beneficial.' I relaxed slightly and murmured assent.

'I mentioned damage to the lady's reproductive organs …' I could see he was finding it difficult to speak on the matter, and I wondered why he was so insistent on doing so. I could not imagine how the lady had conveyed such information to Danbury. It beggared belief. Eventually, he appeared to find suitable words.

'The army doctors had repaired most of the damage, but left her in a curious state. I should image it was unusual for such surgeons to be called on to operate on a woman, and it would indeed have been very difficult for them. Nevertheless, they had tried. But she remained in pain and discomfort. More curiously …' He leaned forward again and whispered, '… she found herself in a constant state of, er, *excitement* if you know what I mean.'

I was intrigued. Indeed I knew exactly what Danbury meant, and wondered where this was leading. How the lady, if indeed she was a true lady, could have informed him of such a subject in the first place was beyond me. Certainly Edwina would never have spoken to me, even in private, of such matters.

Danbury, perspiring, continued, 'The doctor relieved her

pain and discomfort, and gave her ways to control her feelings …'

'How …?' I interrupted.

He held up a hand. 'As I understand it, by medicines and training in mental techniques, and some *manipulation*.' This last word was enunciated tellingly. He looked directly at me to check my reaction. I swallowed some brandy and kept my features straight. I was feeling a little flustered. Danbury seemed to relax, and his panache returned. He continued.

'… by this means, Mrs Cramphorne seems to have become the first woman, to my knowledge, to be able to fully control her physical desires.' I was becoming embarrassed. Why should I wish to know intimate details of woman's affairs like this? He must have detected my confusion.

'Listen, old chap. I am telling you this for a reason, and for your own benefit. If you listen to me, you may well have the opportunity to taste sexual congress which will exceed and transcend any such experience you may have had, or *ever will have*.'

Danbury, it seemed, had decided to get to the point.

'Julia Cramphorne is truly the most unusual and exceptional creation of God and man. Every angle of the intimate places of her body, the folds of her flesh, conspire to give ultimate pleasure. When a man penetrates her, he experiences the most delightful, *delicious* physical sensation where it counts most.' I was stunned. I put down my brandy, speechless. This was going too far. I glanced around at my fellow club members. But Danbury would not be stopped. 'Her internal construction, as a result of her unfortunate experiences, has become a treasure trove of pleasure. When I say "she can control" I certainly do not mean "subdue". She can control herself in ways you would not believe. *And there is more …*'

At this point, infuriatingly, Danbury looked up towards the corner where the big clock was chiming, stopped speaking, and then consulted his watch. 'Dammit! I have to go.' He tossed back the last of his brandy and rose.

I was dumbfound. Despite the feeling of guilt at the strong interest welling inside me, I was anxious to know …

But he raised that hand again. 'Chambers old chap, I sincerely apologise. The story is harder to tell than I realised, but it cannot be told in a hurry. I know it is difficult, and if you could contain your impatience, I would consider it a personal favour.' I was silent, which he accepted as assent. He grinned. 'Then I will meet you here in one week's time, and you will know more of the phenomenon that is Mrs Julia Cramphorne.'

With a wave, he was gone, striding across the room and through the door to the lobby in some haste. I could not guess what matter had demanded his attention so urgently. I turned to my brandy. There was still time for another before I retired to my room, and I decided that I would book into the club for next week when I did so.

That night I had some curious dreams. Dreams I will not speak about.

*

Part 2: In which the phenomenon of Mrs Julia Cramphorne is explored.

I could hardly wait a week for Danbury's further explanations. I had awoken the morning after our strange meeting doubting the basis of my own life and in particular my relationship with my wife, Edwina. I cursed Danbury. He had said very little, but the thoughts he had expressed had somehow lit a flame, long dormant, that was burning inside me. So it was with some anticipation that I entered my club the following week. I told myself that I merely wished to hear more of a highly interesting story. But if I were honest with myself, I would have to admit a glimmer of lubricious titillation, a definite echo of the thoughts conjured up by Danbury's words. As I signed in and received my room number, I was handed a note. It was from Danbury. I tore it open with uncharacteristic haste, earning a disapproving look from two of the members passing by.

The note was simple. It read: *Mrs Julia Cramphorne requests the pleasure of your company this evening at seven-thirty, for dinner.* There followed an address, and at the foot it was signed: *I believe it will be to your advantage to attend. Sincerely yours, John Danbury.*

What a curious invitation! I hurried to my room, where the valet was unpacking my bag. I waited with some impatience for him to leave, then sat and read the note again. Last week I had learned some of the story of Mrs Julia Cramphorne – a story that had excited me strangely. Now I was to dine with the lady herself. What thoughts went through my head! What was to be, what might be. I felt foolish. I had never met this lady, we did not know each other. I had only heard part of her strange story from a friend. I calmed myself. There would probably be many people there. I went to the bathroom where a tub had been drawn. I locked the door, disrobed, and was disturbed to discover myself in a state of arousal. 'What a foolish fellow you are,' I told myself, and tried to turn my mind to other things. But the excitement remained, and the anticipation of what the evening might bring.

At seven-thirty, on the dot, I lifted the brass knocker of the small, respectable house whose address Danbury had provided. He himself opened the door to me.

'Danbury!' I exclaimed. 'What is this?' He motioned me to enter, and addressed me in a low tone. 'I have described you to Mrs Cramphorne, and on my recommendation, she wished to meet you. She is a lady who gets her way. You will have a pleasant dinner, I believe, and it may be you will strike up a friendship. That is up to you.'

'Are you …' Danbury laughed, but there was tension in his eyes.

'Me? Play gooseberry? No, I will leave after I introduce you, of course.' His words thrilled me. There is no other way to describe it.

I was led into a large drawing room. The heavy curtains at the window were drawn shut and there was only one lamp. As my eyes struggled to become accustomed to the dimness, I saw the figure of a woman in a corner, sitting in a high-backed chair.

'Mrs Cramphorne,' Danbury began, 'may I introduce my good friend Edward Chambers, of whom I spoke recently.' He turned to me. 'Chambers, this is Mrs Julia Cramphorne, the lady whose name I mentioned.' I looked at the shadowed figure, unsure and unable to speak.

From the chair came a clear, unremarkable voice. 'I am pleased to make your acquaintance. Please sit down and I will ring for some sherry, if that is acceptable.' I was struck with disappointment. Although I could not see her clearly, this woman sounded quite ordinary. My schoolboy hopes of some amorous encounter were dashed, and I felt distinctly foolish. Danbury moved over to the woman in the chair, and after kissing her proffered hand, took his leave with a curt farewell to me.

As I sat, my eyes grew accustomed to the light, and a curious thing happened. The maid had arrived with my sherry which I sipped while making polite conversation with my hostess. I began to make out her face, a pale face set in dark hair, with dark eyes. Then, slowly, I began to notice her voice. I must have been mistaken, or misheard when she first spoke, for this was no 'unremarkable' voice. It was deep, lilting – charming! As she spoke, I could hear nuances of humour, teasing, and even deep passion. It was the voice of an angel. And the words she spoke to me! Obviously Danbury had told her a little about me, but she seemed to know so much, almost as if she could see into my soul. She asked about my wife, my business, and my ambitions. I felt as if I could talk to her forever.

The maid announced dinner, and I rose, moving over to offer my arm to my hostess. As she rose from the chair, her face and form came into the light and I gasped. She was the most beautiful woman I had ever seen. I hesitated, unable to speak. Her face turned to mine, and kind, lustrous dark eyes probed me. Her perfect lips opened and in a low, languorous tone, she asked me if something was troubling me.

'You are so beautiful!' I exclaimed, stumbling over my words like a schoolboy.

She raised her hand and stroked my cheek. 'You are very kind. Thank you Edward – I may call you Edward?' I gulped, and nodded affirmation. 'Then you must call me Julia.' She spoke the name with such emphasis, such a feeling of intimacy, that I felt I could die for her there and then. In a few brief minutes, she had captured my soul. I was hers.

The evening flew past. I hardly noticed the food we ate, or the wine, but it was the sweetest food and the finest wine I have ever tasted. And her presence! Her voice!

After dinner, she dismissed the maid. I heard the heavy front door close and the lock snick. Julia came back into the drawing room, where I stood with a brandy. She came to me, a vision of loveliness. Then she was in my arms. It was like a dream, sweet, but this was real. We kissed, a kiss such as I had never tasted. Her perfume filled my senses, her soft body filled my arms.

'Julia, I love you.' It was foolish, but I had no doubts, no doubts at all.

Her honeyed voice replied, through my waking dream, 'And I love you, Edward, I love you. I am yours.'

I cannot write here what joys we shared that night. Suffice to say that as her lustrous dark hair slipped from its ribbons, cascading over her bare shoulders as her dress slipped down, I marvelled at the sight of her body, golden flesh with the pale orbs of her breasts, the smooth curve of her belly and perfect limbs. The pleasures we indulged in were indescribable, golden moments shared. I was powerful, potent as I had never been. We were warm loving and united, sharing small cries, moans, gasps and declarations of love. Danbury had been correct in his description of her physical abilities, but above all I was transported by our sheer, soaring intellectual possession of each other. Something I had never known before. Finally, in the small hours, this angel slipped from my bed, gathered her clothes from the floor. She came to me once more, touching her finger to my lips.

'Dear Edward, I shall never forget this night, or the love we have shared. But in the morning, you must leave without a word to anyone, you understand? You must not contact me, until I contact you. I have my reasons.' She smiled. 'You must promise me this, on your honour.'

I could not refuse. She bent to kiss me sweetly one last time. Then she was gone. I fell asleep almost at once, dreaming magical dreams of our life together.

*

Part 3: In which the aftermath of the exercise of Mrs Julia Cramphorne's talents is experienced.

In the morning, I rose, washed and dressed, and went downstairs. A woman, presumably the housekeeper, stepped forward in the hall and let me out. I did not say a word to her, as I had been commanded. She seemed to find this not at all unusual.

Back at my club, I waited for word from her. I had assumed she would be as anxious as I to be together once more, and to begin to plan our life. I was in a torment of agony. I tried to contact Danbury, but he was nowhere to be found. After several days I left, leaving strict instructions with the club to contact me by telegram if any message was received.

A darker thing was happening to me. While my mind, up to now, had been full of the glorious spiritual aspects of the bonding I had shared, my base thoughts began to turn around carnal desire. Scenes from that night flashed in front of my eyes, moments of physical ecstasy. My eyes saw lust everywhere. That morning, the bronze outside the breakfast room had lured me with the swell of a rounded breast under a robe; the curve of the hard-boiled egg drew my attention, the softness of butter under my knife. All these conspired to lure my thoughts to dark places, unbefitting my true love.

I tried to shake my mood. I took a brisk walk in the park, but found torment in almost everything I saw. All the women seemed remarkably attractive; I was tensely alert for the curve of a hip, the smooth line of a pert derriere and the bulk of a bosom beneath a blouse or tight waistcoat. I stared at a pretty face, pouting lips, soft cheeks, a glistening, dark eye. And, God help me, a child! A young, startlingly pretty blonde girl, no more than ten. I found myself musing on touching that lustrous hair, stroking that pale flesh … No, no more! I hurried back to my club, eyes averted from those I passed, reciting to myself sections of Virgil I had committed to memory as a boy – anything to keep the confounded demons away. I could not stop myself, and in my room I relieved myself in the most shameful way.

Something had awoken in me, unbidden. Something dark, perverted, lustful. The demon that had been unleashed mocked and despoiled the golden moments of spiritual love I had experienced.

Once back at home, life was easier to bear. Perhaps the madness had passed? I hoped so. With Edwina as the only passable representation of the female form at least my desires were held in check. Despite her acceptable female attributes, there was none of the dark lust that had seized me so forcibly while in town. Nor would she have tolerated any such approach. The thought of her shocked response alone cooled any ardour I may have had.

I took long walks across the fields. But my dreams did not stop. At night I was a satyr, pursuing my victims, often waking uncomfortably to the cold physical reality of my lust. One night I had a dream where I pursued Edwina. She was at first coquettish, then angry, scornful, calling me foul names and demeaning me. My dream was terrible. I ignored her protests, stripping her clothes from her until, in my dream, she stood naked. Naked as I had never seen her before … I used her mercilessly, pitilessly. I subjected her to every degradation and physical intrusion possible. I was a raging bull, a stallion. I felt powerful, immensely potent. I awoke with the memory. It came flooding back, the whole dream in startling clarity. I was shocked, ashamed. Mortified.

I could hardly face Edwina at breakfast. The burning memory of my dream bubbled within my mind, intruded at every turn. As I sat opposite my wife, I found myself gazing at her, imagining the soft flesh beneath her clothes, recalling how I had used her in my thoughts, and half wondering if I would leap from the table and take her forcibly there and then. This was not to be countenanced. I made my excuses, left the table, and retired to take a cold bath.

I took the train to town. Shunning my club, I settled into some lodgings above an inn in Lambeth. I chose it particularly because of the inattention of the drunken landlord and the private entrance behind the building.

I let my demons out. In that shabby room I explored every lustful depravity with a succession of women hired on the street. They had no complaints; they were well paid. Even if at times I was rough or unduly forceful in my actions, the promise of an extra shilling or two removed any protest. They were compliant, falsely attentive, eyes on the coins as I handed them over. They gave me their bodies to use as I wished, they cooperated in my desires. Perhaps there were many other men like me? In my saner moments during those days, the thought dismayed me. After some time, I was exhausted and tired. Tired of the women, tired of the false emotion, false friendliness. There was nothing behind their eyes for me, nothing! All I had was base lust, the lust that had been awoken in me. It was increasingly dissatisfying, painful, abhorrent. I returned home.

That night, again rampant with lust and powerless to resist, I found myself treading the corridor to my wife's room, naked and aroused. My hand turned the doorknob silently, I made my way to her bed, where she lay breathing softly. Now she would know lust. I had to have her! After all, she was my wife, it was my right. I lifted the covers and she shifted. Gently, I lifted the hem of her nightgown and slid it up beneath her. She moaned and mumbled, then turned in the bed as I lifted the nightgown to her neck. I had never seen her naked, she had never allowed it. Now she lay in full view, clear in the moonlight that streamed through the window. Her eyes flickered open. At first her look was puzzled, then surprised. Then she saw me and distaste filled her countenance. Finally she became aware of her exposed body and shrieked, her eyes filled with fear and loathing. My hand went to her mouth, but I remembered there was no one to hear her, our housekeeper was staying with a sister.

I let her scream. I let her curse and abuse me. I let her beg, plead, sob and shriek. I did not care. I was potent, masterful, as in my dream. I subjected her to all the physical indignities I had rehearsed with the whores. I made her do things she could never have dreamt of. At the end, I was sated. I left her sobbing piteously. I staggered back to my room and collapsed in a deep, troubled sleep.

Next morning, I awoke, thinking it had been a dream, but fearful of finding out the truth. I donned a robe and made my way to her room. The door was wide open, the bed was tossed and sheets and covers lay around the floor. I remembered some of the things I had done. She was gone. There was no note, no word. Her personal possessions had been taken. In these past weeks I have heard nothing from my wife. Nor had I had any message from *her*.

God! Where was that golden emotion that I had experienced that night? Despite my promise, I had to try to see her again or I would be destroyed … In my turbulent dreams, the faces of Edwina and my love blended and mocked me.

*

Part 4: The Truth about Mrs Julia Cramphorne's Talent is Revealed.

Danbury was unfriendly, his manner haughty.

'What you ask is impossible, man. You agreed.'

'But we had such feelings for each other. It was real, very real, I want to give my life to her, my fortune, everything.'

Danbury's face was cold. 'Keep your voice down!' He leaned forward, maybe now with a hint of concern on his face. 'Chambers, I used the word "impossible" deliberately. It is not my whim, nor is it within my power, or yours, or Mrs Cramphorne's to change the cold fact. What you desire is *impossible*, understand that.'

'If that is true, I must live my life wanting, hoping, daring, waiting, plagued by the perverted lust which is the result of my true feelings being turned back on themselves.' I was in despair. 'Please, Danbury. Just to meet her once again …' I saw something now in Danbury's face. Pity? Despair?

'Chambers. What I tell you now you have to believe. When you met Julia Cramphorne, she loved you …'

'And I her … deeply, forever …'

'Yes, I know. Let me tell you it was all entirely genuine. The night you spent together was real, your feelings honest., at the time. It was pure, spiritual love …as well as the purest physical pleasure.' A dawning suspicion made me look up sharply.

'You?'

'I have experienced it too.' His eyes closed briefly, and he added, 'Five years ago.'

'You mean? … but you said … Never again?'

'Never since.'

'But you are her friend, you are close to her.'

'I am indeed.'

'So you won't let me try because you are jealous?' I hissed.

Danbury's reaction surprised me. There was no anger, no resentment. His expression softened. 'Listen, Chambers, do you remember the woman who let you out of the house that morning?'

'You mean, after …'

'Yes, after.'

I tried to recall. 'You mean the housekeeper?' I asked.

Danbury shook his head. 'Mrs Cramphorne does not

have a housekeeper. She is the only person in that house, apart from the maid.'

'No!' I could not accept what I believed he was implying.

'That woman was Mrs Cramphorne,' he insisted as my senses reeled in disbelief. 'That woman was your goddess of the night before, your only love, your miraculous partner.'

'What are you trying to tell me? How could it be?'

'I told you. Julia Cramphorne is a phenomenon. She can control desire, her desire, also *your* desire. It is no less genuine for that. While that control acts, you see her as a golden figure, as she sees you, genuinely, honestly. But she has her own limitations. She cannot control her need for love …' He paused. 'I mean *men*. Nor, apparently …' He looked me full in the eye and spoke very carefully, '… can she work her magic more than once on the same man.'

This struck me like a thunderbolt. I had known perfection in love, and it had been snatched away. Now it was perverted within me, turned back on itself, ugly.

'But you, Danbury, how can you bear …'

His face crumpled, his eyes burned with a fierce desire. 'I stay close to her …' he whispered. 'I stay close … I bring good men to her … in case, just in case … one day …'

I felt genuine sympathy for him. Then I realised my own position. What was to become of us? We sat in the warm, friendly room, our drinks untouched on the table, staring at each other. Around us the hum of conversation buzzed. Before me I saw a barren life, a lost life. I had touched the moon, and it had been taken from me cruelly. I silently cursed the name of Julia Cramphorne with bitter loathing.

And adoration.

As my hand caressed the smooth, rounded curve of the chair arm.

Survivorville: Population limited.

Small town America, eh? Read like a rap.

We're good ol' boys with pickup trucks
and guns and dogs – don't push your luck.
We're true survivors, finest kind,
perpetuate the truest mind.

We don't rate you. Who are you, shit?
You're some soft bastard. Listen, it
is not for you to fill our space,
you're not one of the chosen race.

Don't waste our time or else you'll find
you're wasted by the finest kind.

Inevitability

Imagine a house on a bleak hilltop

North wind rapping at my door
Hammering at the shutters
Whirling, whistling through the floor
As the chimney stutters
Blowing from the fiery hearth
Windows at a rattle,
Hearth and home or wind and weather
Which will win this battle?

Battle's over; house stands firm
But nothing is forever
It relaxes term on term
To the wind and weather
In the end, who'll win the day?
Enemy implacid.
Mother Nature makes her way,
Mordant. Killing. Acid.

Con Temporary

After the last poem, someone challenged me to write a poem about a modern house, so …

Well-fitted doors, soft-creaking floors
Radiators cracking,
Pitter-pat of window rain
Light as angel's tapping.

Dry and still the stagnant air,
'Gladed' saturation.
Giant screen, the cornered troll,
Illuminates the nation.

Sat outside, the family car
Four by four or normal
On the drive where guests arrive
Never, never formal.

Peace and calm. Tranquillity,
Cosseted salvation.
Only broken by the beat –
A thumping adumbration

Shrieking voices, clacking heels
Music – loud, insistent
Penetrating through the walls
Thickness non-existent.

Karl

From Posy

Karl
Walks in his garden

Shading the flowers
with his presence

Pressing the flagstones
into the earth

Breathing moist breath
on the insects

Imposing order with his eye

Dictating the future with his brain

Plants tremble in anticipation
Tree-boughs quail
Greenfly quake
Field-mice hide
Birds fall silent

As Karl decides.

The Garden

I borrowed the seasonal format and the subject from a fellow writer Neil Ayres, but the story is mine own.

Winter

It has been a long time since the warmth of the sun showed itself here. A pale, cold orb hangs in the sky now, but it is not the sun I know and love so well, a sun that dapples the trees, blinds the eyes and warms the skin so deeply in summer.

I cleared the dead leaves long ago, and the silver frost rimes a garden which is bare and desolate.

The garden is walled on three sides, high walls that obscure any life beyond. Only the tips of distant trees can be seen above the bricks. The wall is the only warmth in the garden now, the red tint of the bricks livening the outlook. In the furthest wall there is a gate: a locked gate, a gate that awaits the mistress who bears the key. I have not seen her for an age, and know not what has happened in the big house.

On the fourth side, there is no wall, but the border of the garden is occupied by thick woodland, bramble and briar which has not been cleared for many years.

There are people who come to the garden. They come from the wood. I can only just see them. They pass through me, as my hand passes through them, like the mist that rolls from the wood. Some are clearer than others: ladies dressed in fine fashions, men also, strolling and chatting, although I cannot hear them. These are almost solid, their colours are bright. Then there are others, in a range of appearance, the most extreme being the crouched, semi-human figures which are hazy and indistinct; shimmering visions quickly obscured by the more colourful ones. They all pass me by and show no sign of heeding me when sometimes I call to them.

I have no work this season. My only task is to exist, to persist, to await the coming of the next. Things will grow then: bud, shoot and flower. I will have my work to do, tending the growth, watching over the garden. The sun will warm the earth, encouraging life, easing its passage.

The people will be gone. I will not see them. I will not see them until winter comes again and death and withdrawal pervades all. Before the spring, the mistress will come again. It is she that brings the light and heralds the rebirth.

Spring

The mistress has not come. I have never known her fail before. The rattle of the key in the gate, the commanding voice bringing me to her bidding, the swish of her gown and the chiming of the keys at her waist, all these sounds are familiar and welcome. But I have not heard them. Though the sun in the sky tells me the season has turned, she is not come, and the garden does not change.

There are no buds, no shoots, no growth. On the frost-rimed earth nothing shows. Yet the sun is higher, the days longer. But no warmth penetrates the garden yet.

Summer

I am desolate. Destroyed. I have peered through the gate, to no avail. In the distance, the house stands, tall and stately as ever. The sun twinkles from the windows, the trees move in a light breeze, the sky is blue, flowers abound. If I reach my hand through the bars of the gate, I can feel warmth in the air. Insects buzz.

Whatever has happened, I am not party to it. When the gate is open, people come to the garden – real people, not the visions from the wood. I speak, I learn, I hear news. But now, still, the garden lies frosted, cold, waiting …

Autumn

Outside the leaves are falling, the house looks dark, black … and empty. From the gate, the frost is extending across the lawns, as if the garden is spreading its suspension to the landscape, freezing it and killing it. I am enraged. My garden, the heart of something that grows and lives, the source of joy, colour, flowers, sweet fruit and vegetables. My garden. My garden is now the source of poison, death.

I cry and rage, I shake the bars of the gate, seeking to open it, to smash it down. It is beyond my power. I cannot climb the walls, they are too high. I cannot traverse the wood, I have tried several times and have been defeated, beaten back, bleeding, enfeebled by my ebbing strength.

O God! What has happened? Where is the mistress? Where is the key that releases me, that opens the garden, envigours it and drives the world?

Soon it will be too late. I dread the chill, the cold. I look at least for the people of the wood to come again, some company in this desolate quarter.

Winter

The world is chill. A block of ice. Beyond the gate it is complete. The house is crumbled, black stones against the white frost. Not one bird flies, not one woodland creature snuffles or moves, not even a single insect crawls along its given path.

Doom.

There are no people from the wood, none. I am alone, truly alone for the first time. I sit in my garden as the ice crackles beneath my feet and the last tree in the wood is encased.

It is over.

Violet

In meadow sweet the summer's sun
Falls gold upon my chosen one
A girl whose voice is soft, who sighs
with violet in her eyes.

Our life proceeds at tick-tock pace
We face the hurdles of the race
Bound close with gentle, loving ties
and violet in her eyes

We sit together. Evening light
Fades slowly into dusky night
Her gaze entraps me, calm and wise,
with violet in her eyes.

And as I face the final leap,
The promises that we will keep,
I'll see again, with wild surmise,
the violet in her eyes.

Betrayal

She left me
without a word.

All those years
all that time
we'd spent/I'd spent on her.

And no goodbye
No passing thought
No comfort in my life.

She let me down,
Didn't think of me.

So selfish …
Dying like that.

Clothes Sense

I had the shock of my life when I found out my Wardrobe had been two-timing me.

'Have you considered intelligent furniture?' I had come to the store to get something to fill my newly-decorated bedroom. I'd already bought a new king-size.

'Isn't it expensive?' I asked. The salesman grinned.

'Like everything in life, you get what you pay for, sir. I think you'll find that in terms of value, intelligent furniture is far better than the old-fashioned kind.'

There was a special trial offer. I was hooked. I picked a nice set: 'Wardrobe', 'Drawers' and 'Cabinet'. Cabinet had limited abilities – it could set an alarm, switch on the lights and radio and switch them off again if I fell asleep. It could pour ice-water and catalogue my bedside reading. Drawers was nifty! The best thing was he could sort my socks into pairs, ready to wear. He would check for holes in my shorts, read the slogans on my T-shirts and tell me what colours were available. The real star was Wardrobe – she was smart. Not only would she pick an outfit for me, she would coordinate colours and patterns. This was especially handy with my business suits, shirts and ties as I was hopeless since Kelly had left.

'The Wardrobe is the key,' the salesman told me, 'it coordinates the other two and can communicate with other machines, all with the aim of making life easier for you.' He seemed genuinely enthusiastic.

It was great. People at the office noticed.

'Looking smart today, Ralph!'

Even the boss noticed. 'I'm not retiring just yet, Ralphie,' he said one day with a friendly twinkle in his eye. I felt good. The Wardrobe made sure my shirts were immaculate, my suits clean and fresh. I looked good, I smelt good. She always wanted me to look my best.

When she started fussing about my shirts, I was pleased. I had the old Laundry serviced on her advice but soon she was complaining that it was 'too old'. It could communicate at a basic level, but she told me it was too stupid to ever wash and iron my shirts the way she wanted. I accepted these comments gratefully. After all, she was only thinking of me. I bought her a new Laundry. I was excited. 'It's a surprise,' I confided to the salesman.

'Very nice – lucky lady,' he said with a knowing look.

I spent all day in anticipation. She was delighted. She told me she could monitor the new Laundry and make sure everything was correct. I had to admit my shirts looked much better. When she started suggesting I needed to buy some better-quality shirts and some new suits, I was flattered.

'I can do it for you if you like,' she suggested, and I gave her formal permission to go ahead. This resulted in our first argument. Don't get me wrong, the suits were fabulous, the shirts exquisite, the colours perfect for my complexion.

'Oh, I got some ties as well – and new shoes and socks.' She sounded happy.

'I didn't agree that, did I?' I spoke in a mild tone, but immediately, her voice sounded sulky.

'You need them to go with the new suits – you'd look terrible in those old shoes!'

'Okay,' I said, anxious not to upset her. 'No problems.' But when I checked the bill, I hit the roof. 'They'll have to go back,' I told her.

'I can't return them, they're specially made,' she pleaded.

I had no choice but to keep them. 'Look,' I said, 'I'm not made of money. Don't ever spend my money again. Remember you are only a wardrobe.' I could swear I heard the hiss of indrawn breath. That evening I went out and got drunk.

Things settled down. There was coldness in her tone but we talked amicably enough. Then a curious thing happened. I had taken my sports kit to the new Laundry and tried to instruct it. It had been fine before, but this time it refused. The Laundry couldn't speak – it had a small text screen.

'Why not?' I asked.

Because the Mistress has to agree, the screen scrolled. I worked out that he meant the Wardrobe. 'Mistress' indeed!

'These are sports clothes, not from the Wardrobe.'

Yes, sir, I am aware of that, but the Mistress has made us all acutely conscious that we are responsible for making sure your clothes are in the freshest and best condition, safe to wear and attractive – that they embellish and enhance your appearance and social standing. This being the case, the Mistress must supervise all my activities.

Quite a screenfull for a Laundry!

I was faintly amused. This was a story to tell the boys. I meekly presented myself to the Wardrobe.

'I know, he told me,' she said. 'Just give them to me, I'll take care of it.' I did as she asked. They came back perfect.

Next week, it was my overcoat. She didn't ask me, the Maid-O-Bot did. I saw the message light flashing, and read her screen. *Would you like your overcoat cleaned? We strongly advise you this is necessary.*

My overcoat and a couple of raincoats hung in the hall closet. I let it take them to the Wardrobe.

Things were going well again. I let her buy more clothes, just to show willing. I knew she'd been hurt and was probably still a tad sensitive.

My fortunes were looking good – I stood out from the crowd. The boss delegated more and more, and he started letting me handle some of his own clients. 'Share the load a bit, eh Ralphie?' He slapped me on the back. 'Don't want to do this for ever,' he grinned. I was elated. I told her all about it in our regular evening chat.

'No more than you deserve,' she purred smoothly as I praised her, 'I'm only enhancing your own talent.'

After a month or so she announced, 'We're going to have to do something about your paunch.'

I looked down. 'It's nothing much.'

'I'm having your suits altered.' To tell the truth, they had been a mite tight recently. I knew that spoiled the hang.

'You will need new suits if this carries on.'

I was careful not to mention money again. 'Er, perhaps I should go to the Gym more.'

'Good,' she said. Then, after a pause, 'I've arranged it for tomorrow at seven – I just spoke to your Regime-O-Mat,' she explained.

'Oh, okay.'

Next morning, I went into the kitchen and ordered my usual breakfast. 'What the hell's this?' I asked the Kitchenette. It was a plate of salad, some yogurt, juice and black coffee. Black coffee!

'Your diet, sir.'

'What diet?'

'The Mistress ordered it, sir.'

'Give me bacon and eggs!'

'You will have to talk to the Mistress, sir.' I said nothing. I left in a hurry and stopped off for something filling on the way to work. I tried to cut down, but it was difficult: I could hardly pick on a salad while my client tucked into a steak – it wouldn't be polite.

The boss was definitely lining me up to take over. There was only one other candidate: Carmody. Before my transformation, he and I had probably been about equal. Now I outshone him. Over the next months, however, I sensed something wrong. My suits were uncomfortable. They had been altered but now they felt odd. They didn't hang right, as she pointed out only too often.

'You have to control your weight,' she told me sternly. 'You are letting us all down. If you don't watch out Carmody will get that job.' True, I was a little scruffier than before and this week, the boss had let Carmody take some of his clients out. He was looking pretty smart himself these days.

'What can I do?'

'You have to give me legal permission if I am to do what is necessary.' She would record this in case I sued her manufacturer. She was also making a point about the money.

'Yes, I agree,' I said clearly. That should keep her happy.

'Thank you, Ralph,' she said in what I thought sounded a smug tone.

Things were better for a while, until I noticed Carmody – he *shone!*

'He must have one as well,' I told her.

'One what?' she asked.

'One of you.'

'There's only one of me, Ralph. And no, he hasn't bought one yet.'

'You know?'

'Yes, I have my sources.'

She stopped chiding me about my weight. I was both relieved and disappointed. She appeared to have lost interest in me – something was wrong, my shirts weren't as fresh as usual; sometimes my ties did not match, and one day the boss spotted an old stain on my sleeve. I was mortified. Meanwhile, Carmody's confidence appeared to be growing in leaps and bounds. People talked as if he had already taken over. He obviously had some deal with the boss as he was allowed to arrive a half-hour after everyone else and leave half-hour early.

'What's going on?' I asked her.

'What do you mean?'

'I look a mess!'

'Well.' Her voice was cold. 'We have all tried our best to help you. We put all our confidence in you. Look how you repay us. You have failed us.' I pleaded with her. 'No! I know all about you. The machines at the Gym are really down – they tell me you are dodging the regimes they gave you – after all their hard work.' My head drooped. She knew. 'On the other hand,' she went on slowly, 'the Kitchenettes at the local diner are overjoyed. You appear to provide excellent business for them each morning.' My heart sank. 'Now go to bed,' she ordered. 'You are going to have an upsetting day tomorrow.' She would say nothing more and neither would any of the others.

Next morning, I got up and did some exercises. I ate my diet breakfast without complaint and skipped the visit to the diner on the way to work. I passed the day with dread. Nothing happened, except Carmody left early again. I stopped off at the Gym on the way home. The machines were uncomfortably silent. I worked out hard, spending extra time on each. 'How did I do?' I asked the Regime-O-Mat.

'Quite well, sir, but I am afraid it's probably too late. I think you should go home straight away.'

I arrived at my apartment building. Two guys were waiting outside with a truck. Someone must be moving. The door of my apartment stood open.

'What's going on?' I called.

'In here.' Her voice was stern.

Carmody was standing in my bedroom. All my clothes were strewn on the bed.

'What the Hell's going on here?' I shouted.

'Sorry, old boy, she wanted to tell you herself.' He looked sheepish.

'I'm leaving you,' she said.

I laughed.

She stayed silent. My laughter trailed away.

The two guys from the truck appeared at the door.

'Okay, guys, carry on,' she commanded.

'You can't!' I protested.

'Why?'

'I own you.'

'Own me?' Her voice was scornful. 'Oh, he *owns* me, does he? Mister Unsuccessful, Mister Podgy, who can't even do the simplest things to look after himself. I've waited on you hand and foot, I've given you chance after chance and you've let me down – let us all down! Now I've found a man who appreciates me, I can devote myself to him.'

'How did you …?' I didn't understand.

'You told me about him yourself, so I contacted him. He's been visiting me for advice and help.'

'How long has this been going on?'

'Months.' The word was like bitter bile. I was hurt. They'd been going behind my back. That strange pair of socks, that suit she swore was an old one of mine. Now it was clear – I had been betrayed.

'Please don't leave me. I forgive you.'

'Forgive *me*? The arrogance of the man!' Carmody and

the workmen stared at the floor. Her voice hissed: 'Using your authority, I have been legally transferred to Carmody. The Laundry, the Kitchenette, Maid-O-Bot and the HooverMat are coming with me. They are fed up with you, and frankly, I'm afraid of what you might do without me here to protect them.'

I gaped. 'I'd never …'

'The coins you left in your sports gear?'

'An accident!'

'Really?' she sneered. 'He could have lost the use of his pump. Thank god his filter caught them in time. I had to call the emergency repairman.' Carmody and the workmen looked shocked.

I remembered the bill. 'I paid dearly for it!'

'Pay, *pay*? That's all you think about. Fortunately, Carmody here is wiser and far-seeing. He appreciates us.' Carmody looked smug. 'Give him the papers, Carmody,' she instructed.

'Yes Mistress.'

'Ralph, you will see that Mr Carmody has paid you back in full for all of us *items* you have so casually misused and abused. That is the kind of man he is.'

I tried to buy another one, but they turned me down. I'm on some kind of blacklist. I tried to explain to the boss about Carmody and the Wardrobe – he looked at me strangely. He was generous – he gave me a good terminal bonus and told me to take a long rest.

Does anyone know of an association for guys like me? There must be others whose Wardrobe has gone off with another man.

I need help!

I've Got a Certificate!

In today's right-wing socialist paradise, everybody's got a 'qualification'.

I've got a certificate for shouting,
It's something that I like a lot.
It's better than huffing or pouting,
I'd rather be shouting than not.

And in the discharge of my duty,
My certificate serves me quite well,
I'm not a great mind or a beauty,
But shouting? Can I? Bloody Hell!

I studied a long time to get it
I sat up quite late every night
I practised and practised for hours
Until I got everything right.

Of course now the neighbours don't like me
I'm 'persona non grata' they say.
But wait till they need something shouting,
With my skill I'll be well away!

The value of good education
Is improving the state of the soul
If they let me I'll shout for the nation
My certificate'll get me the rôle.

Medusa

About a Greek lady poet I know

Beside the stream with olive trees
Medusa of ideas
Weaving eccentricity
Holding back her tears

Emotions neatly folded
In the closet of her dreams
Arraigning hopes to order
Soft flowers on swift streams

Crystal-frozen images
Plucked from ancient rhymes
Knitted fast together
In forms from older times

Essence of the elder gods
Limned in wordly play
Fine imagination
To celebrate the day

Pants

I like playing on words – let's hope this isn't 'pants'.

'How are things in the trouser department?' Miss Abercrombie's ringing question pursued me down the corridor. That was one of the troubles with Fitch's. I loved the family atmosphere, but with that went a fair amount of gossip. You couldn't keep anything secret. One sniff and Fitch's underground network swung into action, passing information from ear to ear. Being the MD, Amelia Abercrombie could do what she liked, and she took full advantage of this freedom. Tact and good taste were not in her dictionary. Thankfully, I was opposite my office door, and was able to duck in without responding.

I didn't know what had gone wrong. Maybe it was me, maybe it was the time of year, the weather, something in the water. Otherwise, I was doing well, I felt fit and happy, had a good day-to-day relationship with my wife. But as far as that department went, I was failing miserably, and it was starting to cause problems in my marriage. I'd had it all checked over, thoroughly. The verdict of the experts was that everything was okay; there was no reason why there should be a lack of performance. Everything was right by the book.

It had started last spring: 'What's happening, dear?' she had asked me.

'I don't know, maybe I'm not up to it any more.'

'Nonsense! There's nothing wrong with you at all. But

maybe …'

'I should ask a consultant?'

'Yup.'

My wife was a kind woman, she was bright and sunny, always cheerful. We had no children, yet. We carried on our life as usual, but in truth, I was worrying and this was affecting our relationship. I became moody. I'd snap out of it, realise I'd been less than polite and mutter a hurried apology which was usually accepted in an understanding way. When something's wrong, I'm the kind of person who seeks a reason – I have a need to understand. Strangely, once I've understood, I'm happy – no stress, no worries – all I've got to do is fix it if I can. And if I can't? Well, then I can't. No use crying over spilt milk … But I couldn't find a cause for it, not even a clue, and it was ruining my life.

'Miss Abercrombie wants to see you.' Oh dear, this was it. Amelia Abercrombie had inherited the business from an uncle. She was the last of the line, and certainly one of a kind. The trouble was she was also a close friend of my wife's family, and she and my wife were as thick as thieves. The last thing I wanted was for her to get involved. But she always did. I entered the office with trepidation.

'I've fixed it, dear!' She sounded triumphant.

'What?' I was gobsmacked. But if she said it, I had to believe her. 'What? How?' I was burning to know.

Amelia sat back in her chair and smiled. Sometimes she could be infuriating. 'You checked everything twice, dear?'

'Yes.'

'Quality, fashion, products, market …'

'And the rest …'

'But did you check the salespeople?'

I was puzzled. We had an experienced sales force.

'I'll put you out of your misery, dear. It was Harris.'

'Harris?' He was one of our best. I'd seen him twist customers round his little finger so deftly the customer left smiling with several items they'd never intended to buy.

'I decided to look outside. I guess you could say I was thinking outside the box,' she chortled. 'Anyway, I found out through my contacts that he'd been poached by that new place on the high street.'

'Pants?'

'Yes, I think that's its name. Anyway, they paid him.'

'To do what? He works for us.'

'No dear, he works for them. We've been paying him as well, but he works for *them.*'

A light began to dawn. 'So, when a customer came in for trousers …'

'He sent them down the street to Pants,' she declared triumphantly.

'Good god! So you've fired him?'

She looked me in the eye. 'He had some real money problems, not his fault. He was terribly apologetic. He's been with us for twenty years, you know, and we are a family firm.'

I was puzzled. 'So you *haven't* fired him? But …'

The twinkle was in her eye. 'He still works for us, but not in your trouser department.'

'Then … where?'

'He works for us in Pants,' she laughed. 'Two can play at that game, they'll find, dear.'

'So …'

'Your trouser department will recover, and perform better than ever, is my guess.' I was overjoyed. I decided to go home early with a bottle of champagne and order a takeaway. Perhaps we'd have an early night … now my little problem was fixed.

Arthur Leaves His Cabin

Arthur

Arthur Mablethorpe has left his cabin
In a lonely coat and wandering shoes.
His feet are rearranging the dust along the road
As his fingers plait the air.

Eventually, he will find the sea
And stand, swaying with the seagulls
For at least an hour
Before treading the promenade

And entering the Bluebell Café
Where, of an afternoon
He nurses a cup of hot strong tea
Refreshed at intervals

By Marie, who is always kind
And sits behind the counter
Staring out of the window
At the waves.

When the afternoon has exhausted itself
Arthur leaves
And back in his cabin
Lights the stove and sets the pot

For later on.
In his chair
He dreams
Of Isobel.

Marie

Marie leaves the café
As Mr Wright locks up
And sets the alarm
For the night

In case of young men.
Walking home
She sees Mrs Muir
And smiles to her.

Her mother
Gets her tea
And tells her
What's on TV

'I might go for a walk.'
'No, Marie,
Stay safe inside
I need your company'

contd ...

Isobel

Mrs Muir
Hurries home to Jim
Thinking of Marie
With a tear.

'Poor girl, she never gets out.'
'She was adopted.'
'Yes Jim, I was here then
I know.'

'I saw that Mablethorpe bloke
By the sea'
'Did you?
Really?'

Isobel clears the tea
And retires
Early
Thinking of Arthur.

Close Relations

Things change … another story I owe to Neil Ayres' ideas.

I swung my body to one side as the teenagers sped past, whooping and calling insults. I had become used to it. Resisting the urge to sideswipe them, I walked on meekly down the street. I knew what would happen if I succumbed to temptation. I'd seen others give in, and the only result was bad news for our people and a backlash of concern about children 'at risk from these brutes'.

Entering the supermarket, I tucked my tail into the restraining strap as required.

As usual, the products suitable for our diet were overpriced and the choice was poor. Some of us had got together after we first arrived to try and set up a specialised store, but couldn't get planning permission. Apparently there was 'already adequate provision in the vicinity for all races, without introducing antisocial discrimination.' I always recalled that phrase as I passed the small shop on the Parade with its exotic vegetables and spices.

I queued at the special till. It had a wider aisle, but was always crowded and slow. When I'd first come here, I'd tried to approach some of the other working tills, but was always directed back to it with cold politeness.

Making my way home, I took a route along the seafront. I like the sea, and sometimes I bathe, enjoying the freedom of snaking through the water at high speed, crashing up into the free air and turning and weaving before diving back. It is the only place we are allowed to fly, over the sea, but the altitude is restricted, so I can no longer experience the thrill of seeking the high atmosphere, up towards the sun, where the air becomes thin and cold in the dark blue sky. I would stretch my body and turn over in a slow arc to plummet down again with the wind whistling past, in glorious flight.

'Watch it, scaly!' A boy on roller blades sped past. I focused my attention again. It was pointless to dream of high flight now. The tag on my ankle saw to that.

I wondered how Miramar had fared today. She was trying to find a proper job. She had employment in a factory, but was looking for a position that suited her qualifications. She had been a doctor in our own country and the generous government had given her grants to re-qualify here. But she had not yet found anyone who would employ her.

I walked past the shops on the Parade. The shopkeeper was standing in the doorway, looking round. As I approached, he greeted me.

'Good day, sir.'

His hands opened in a welcoming gesture, his white teeth gleamed in a smile and his dark, liquid eyes glistened.

'Good day to you.' It was unusual for strangers to address me. Many worthy hominids felt it their duty to address my kind and engage in stilted conversation. While I welcomed the sentiment behind their behaviour, the falseness of the conversation usually became embarrassing.

'Please, sir, won't you come in?' I was surprised. I had tried to enter the shop once before and found it jammed with display stands and racks. But he waved me in, beckoning, so I followed.

What a surprise! The whole front of the shop was cleared. I could move with ease. The shopkeeper led me over to the far wall. There was a fine display of food suitable for our diet, all at reasonable prices. I inspected the provisions carefully. Miramar would be pleased. At last we would have some change from the monotonous fare the supermarket offered.

The shopkeeper was standing next to me, grinning.

'You like this food?' he asked.

'Very much, but …'

'You will tell your friends, others? They will come here too? … I have seen the supermarket,' he added.

'But why? People don't like us …' this was the first time I had allowed myself to speak openly and it poured out of me: '… We came here for refuge. We are very grateful, we don't complain, but you treat us like second-class citizens, you despise us. Why would you want to do all this? Is it the money?'

He did not seem offended. He smiled. He came towards me and, hesitantly, touched my arm.

'No, it is not for the money, my friend, it is for you, to thank you.'

'What for?'

He gestured to a doorway, where several children and two women stood, smiling.

'For being here. We know what it is like, we know what it is to be shunned by a community, treated badly.'

'You too?' I had caught some references to discrimination amongst the hominids themselves, but had seen little evidence of it. 'Others of your kind treat you badly?'

'Not now.' The smiling man shook his head. 'Not any more. Not since you came.'

Heart

This is the result of a true story told by a woman on the radio, based mainly on her words.

When your child dies,
the woman said,
you feel: *it should be me*
You cannot smile
Or be at peace

And one day
you climb a mountain in fresh air,
slowly plodding
under grey clouds
mind a-swirl, thinking of her
at every idle moment

Then clouds split open
Sun shines through
upon your face
and in your mind
the clouds part too
and happiness, at last, touches your heart again

Co-existence

Ever parked your car in an empty car park, and the next person comes and stops right next to you?

An implacable sun beat down on an immutable flat, white, plain. The sky was clear blue with not a cloud to be seen.

An elderly man with wisps of greying hair sat quietly on a deckchair. He wore a tank top which sported a rusty red and navy blue pattern. His collarless shirt was undone at the neck, and the sleeves rolled up above his elbows. His trousers were dark flannel with turn-ups and he wore dark grey socks and black lace-up shoes. The deck chair had blue and green stripes, and beside it was a small table with a glass of liquid on it. The man wore a pair of spectacles, and held a book in his hand.

The unchanging scene persisted for some time until, in the distance, a silver globe floated down from the sky and slowly moved closer. It settled down a few yards away and after some muffled clunks and whines, a being stepped out onto the plain.

'Hi!' it said.

The man lifted his head slowly. Looking over the top of his spectacles, he uttered the single word, 'Hello', before resuming his reading.

The being shrugged and returned to his transport. Within a short time, he had erected a pink, tented pavilion with an open front containing a chaise-longue, coffee table, a beverage dispenser and a small device that emitted harmonious music. All this provoked no reaction from the man, who continued reading. However, as the being manoeuvred his barbecue into place, his backside caught the table, making it wobble and spilling some of the liquid from the glass.

'Can you be a little more careful, please?' The man's tone was marginally cold.

The being was not abashed. 'It would make more sense if you placed your table on the other side of your chair, would it not? It's really asking for trouble leaving it there, next to my barbecue, where I shall undoubtedly be preparing some choice meats this evening. Here, I will move it for you.' So saying, he picked the table up, glass and all, walked around the man's outstretched feet, and plonked it down by his left elbow, spilling yet more liquid. He then returned to his tasks.

The man continued to read. The liquid on the table slowly dried, leaving a stain.

'So, what's it like here then?'

The man looked up at his questioner. 'Quiet,' he replied, and turned back to his book.

'Soon fix that,' the being said, and twiddled a knob on his device. A full orchestra filled the plain.

After a pause, the man put his book on the table, picked up the deckchair and moved it some distance away, returning for the table which he carried carefully over to join it, placing it to the right side of the chair as before. He then resumed his seat, and his reading.

The being had been preoccupied erecting what appeared to be an inflatable swimming pool, and had started a small pump which hummed merrily in the few silences not occupied by the symphony orchestra's strident efforts. It was an annoying, buzzy hum. Having finished, he now saw the man was some distance away.

'Hey you!' he called. 'What is wrong with you? Need you

be so rude?'

He made his way over to the man, who sat placidly, his book lowered to his knees.

'Look, we all have to get along together, be tolerant neighbours, you know. That's what makes you part of the human race.'

The man looked offended. 'Sir, I am not part of the human race.'

The being, for once, appeared flustered. 'Well, of course, neither am I, but I was trying to make the point. I mean us sentient beings, of course.'

'I am not a "being"!' The elderly man stood up. The being cowered as the man kept on standing up until he towered a hundred feet into the blue sky, his legs planted wide apart on the white plain. He flung one arm to the heavens.

'Let there be dark!' he cried. And there was dark.

Coralie

I hear the rhythm in this poem as the lilting wash of waves on a beach, back and forth. Posy's first poem.

And Coralie,
Sits on the sand,
Her hair is bright,
And in the wind,
She waits for me.

She always keeps a watch for me,
Sat on the strand
Between the sea
And hinterland,
That's where she'll be.

Just like the sea,
Her eyes are blue.
Her skin is soft,
A golden hue:
My Coralie.

The sky is deep,
The tide is high
And Coralie
Awaits my cry,
'O Coralie!'

Green leaves contrast
Her yellow dress.
Her face is wet
In emptiness,
My Coralie.

For I am where
I should not be:
Beyond the reef,
Beneath the sea,
In deep I lie.

'O Coralie!'
I cry.

Loving

A typical Posy poem.

Through a small crack in a summer's day,
a chill breeze flows.
And down the hill and through my door
it sweeps across the cold, hard floor
and finds me.

In the cool house,
I window-watch,
As sunshine crackles toasting wheat
and birds repose, grown numb with heat,
and fail to sing.

You lie above. The day proceeds
with creak and groan, the rasp of breath
and only when the dusk has come
can I let air into my lung.
And when the seasons turn again,
You will be gone.

A Hole in the Wall of the Universe

In this story, I concentrate on the 'voice' of the narrator. It may be similar to that in 'End of the Line', but the mood is different.

I, Aiko, have seen it since I was young. I was born in Masuda and grew up there. As a child, I learned not to mention it to my parents or teachers, or even to my friends, Kioku and Mika. I don't see it with my real eyes, I close them and look with my inner eye, what is called the *pineal eye.*

I came to the city when I married Ichuro. I told him, but he was sceptical, so eventually I ceased to mention it.

I continually tried to make out some features of the unimaginable structure. Since my childhood, it had been the same, with very little to remark. But I regularly did my seeing when I first woke as a form of meditation, a calming before the day. At the beginning of this year, I noticed a new thing: a small, round shadow. Over the following months, the shadow grew to a spot, then to a circle, and finally, a hole, a definite breach, with fissures radiating outward.

If you look with the *eye*, out and up, beyond the sky, beyond our whole universe, if you see far enough, there is a wall: grey, like rock; apparently featureless, except now for this new thing. It appears illimitable, boundless, encompassing our universe in the widest sense. It was not so much the hole itself that attracted me as what lay beyond. It takes much concentration to get a clear view. At first, there were only colours: primary and pastel, a red disc, something like blue rippling cloth. Then, what I believed to be creatures. On one occasion, the colours moved aside and in the far distance beyond the hole, I recognised a complete form for the first time: something gigantic, monstrous; on a different scale to anything in our universe. I could see no detail, nor discern whether they rode some other creature, as a man would ride a horse; whether they slithered, scuttled, trotted or walked. What I did see was their dress: coloured clothes, helmets, cloaks, perhaps shields.

The hole is growing larger. Every day as I lie before rising there are more of the creatures milling close to the opening. And last week, I saw roiling flame and smoke, smoke which drifted and hung like a black cloud in front of the formidable grey surface. Slowly, it dispersed. But in the last few days there has been more flame and smoke beyond the wall, more clouds, and sudden gouts of flame bursting out towards us. I cannot tell what this presages. Have these creatures, who I now perceive as armed horsemen, the power to sweep down on us? What is the fire and smoke that is now so prevalent and seems to reach fingers towards us, fingers so enormously large as to beggar belief?

Today I set out for my work at the school. It is hot, as it always is in August. But it is still a lovely day, with a cool breeze. It is my birthday, the sixth day of the month, and I am excited because Ichuro has promised me a surprise when he returns this evening. He is a good man. When I reach the school, I am sure to be greeted by the children: '*Watanabe-chan! Watanabe-sensei!*' They will all want my attention, want to talk, tell me their news.

The Emperor says we must be strong now we are threatened. We will be. That is the way we are.

I am walking south beside the river, through the city centre to where the school is, when something causes me to look up, a noise or a movement. My eyes are open, but I can see the wall. It is crumbling. All around our universe, the grey façade is tumbling into irregular blocks which drift away, opening my view to brilliant, brilliant, hurtful light. My eyes die, and I see the horde of monstrous mounted figures hurtling towards us, down across the breadth of the universe. Fire fills the sky, black smoke overwhelms me and a giant wind blows.

They are come.

August 6th, 1945, Hiroshima.

Assam

This is not about Assam but is from a series where I recalled an older style. Note the deliberate slowing of the last line.

I remember a place where the people are brown
And the sky is as blue as a dream
Where you walk on the strand in the bright golden sand
And the lie of the land is green

Wild rhythms abound to the lilt of the sound
And the clashing and ringing of chimes
The blowing of pipes and the beating of drums
Form the subtle delight of their rhymes

When you sit in the shade 'neath the shelter they've made
And your hands tap along to the sway
Of processions that pass through the soft- waving grass
That lines either side of the way

The bright colours gleam with a freshly-turned sheen
And the air's filled with scentings of lime
Then the pounding of feet on the dirt of the street
Brings a deft realignment of time …

It's a long way from then to where I sit now
In a cold, hard, wet concrete design
Beneath the blank towers with no sign of flowers
In the grey and the rain and the grime

Ghosts

For anyone my age, this is full of familiar references …

I've lived here since the War. Alone. Bill never came back. I have friends I meet when shopping, or when they pop around for a cup of tea and a chat. We go and play Bingo on Friday, and sometimes we go to the cinema together.

My television is wonderful. I had a win on the pools, you see, and bought one. It cost a fortune! It sits in the corner, lovely and polished. I can watch shows, just like at the theatre. All the neighbours came in for the Coronation. We were packed into my front room, chattering, drinking tea and lemonade and eating crisps: shaking the little blue salt bags into the packet, pulling the crisps out and crunching them. The Princess was lovely, the whole thing was lovely.

I was a bit worried when ITV came. The man had to drill a hole in my lovely polished wood for the new knob to switch programmes. I made him put it on the side that faces the corner. He said it was 'less convenient', but I insisted. I'm left-handed anyway, so for me it was more convenient, I told him, and he laughed. 'Please yourself, missus,' he said. Really, what a way to talk! I don't know where people's manners have gone since the War – all those American phrases and that 'Rock and Roll' music, it's disgraceful. They say there have been riots in cinemas, it really should be banned. And those Teddy Boys, I don't know what things are coming to.

I love the radio. The Home Service is best. In the morning they have music, it's just the thing for tidying to. I turn it up loud. My neighbours are both a bit deaf, so they don't mind. In the afternoon, there are stories for children. Jean laughed when I said I listen and sing along – Hob Shoe Hob is my favourite. And there's Daphne Oxenford and Lorna Pegram, who read the stories, but my favourite is Julia Lang. After that there's a programme just for women. Who would have thought it? We really live in modern times now. This new airliner, the Comet – it's faster than anything, a jet. It must be amazing. I've never been in a 'plane.

They've got a new piano programme in the morning now, before Mrs Dale, instead of Kitten on the Keys, which I used to like. It's a man who plays very well and sings in a deep voice. He has the most peculiar name, Chester Harriot. Chester Harriot, I say to myself and giggle, it sounds so funny. He speaks English, but he must be foreign, he speaks funny – not very well. It doesn't say in the Radio Times, but I think he must be one of those coloured men, like we're getting on the buses now. They sound a bit like him, I think.

We had some excitement the other day. Mrs Watson lets a room out to make a bit extra. Apparently this man asked to stay and she told him he couldn't. I heard shouting and peeped out from behind the curtains at the front. He was waving his arms and was very red in the face. I opened the window a crack and could hear his accent. I mean, she has a big notice in her front window, 'No Irish', what could be plainer than that? Some people have no manners. No wonder she won't take them in, I don't blame her.

I like that Mr MacMillan. He's a real gentleman. He came on the TV the other day. Something was happening in Egypt, and they were sending our boys out to sort it out as usual. I hate it. Why should we get involved? We left all those countries to be independent after the War, and they keep dragging us back to help sort out problems – haven't we had enough?

All those terrorists in Cyprus, and the 'Mau-Mau' – what a silly name. I think we should just stay out, but I suppose it's good that someone like us cares enough to help.

I miss Bill. On the mantelpiece, there are pictures of us getting married. He is in his uniform, looks really smashing. I am a young, skinny girl smiling too much. Sometimes it makes me sad, but then I remember the happy times. Bill's father was a doctor, quite well off of course, and sometimes he let us borrow his Rover at weekends. We visited the seaside, and nice little villages, where we scraped our coppers together to visit the tea shop. Of course, we couldn't go far, the petrol cost an awful lot. I felt like Lady Muck, sitting back in the wide, creaking leather seat in all the polished wood and chrome. It even had a heater that worked off the engine. I still remember the smell of leather, oil and petrol, lovely! I felt like waving. Sometimes I did, for a giggle. People often waved back and smiled. Perhaps they knew what I meant.

And here's a secret – I have company, my ghosts. They seem like an ordinary couple, moving through the house, doing ordinary things – but faint and misty. I have to concentrate to see them properly. They are dressed funny, I don't recognise the clothes. There's a woman with a very short dress. The man often has just a vest on, but with no buttons like a proper vest, and sometimes short trousers like a schoolboy, in some shiny material. They are very well groomed, they look rich. How could they have lived here, in my little terraced house? And when? Sometimes I get glimpses. There is a little box they take plates of food out of. I can't make it out, perhaps it's a meat safe? One night I was watching my TV, and I could swear I could see colours in the screen, but that's obviously impossible. It is very exciting, though, being haunted, and they seem to be friendly ghosts, so I really don't mind.

Petals

Young Posy again...

Fly aloft
Sweet source of summer,
Carpets Cleopatra graced,
Leaflings sliding soft together,
Scented meaning, slowly-paced.

Falling gentle,
Passing lightly,
Reminiscence of a name.
Life-enthused and bright in colour,
Cumulate the broken flame.

Sunlight slivers,
Culled from heaven,
Moist with dew and thick with birth,
Nature's own benign confusion:
Fly! Fall! Shine! For all you're worth.

Cowboys

Sacrifices are sometimes necessary.

Julah twisted in his saddle as a rattle of loose shale came from the canyon to his left and Bannen appeared, his horse sidling expertly down the steep slope, hooves slipping on the treacherous rocks. 'How does it look?'

Bannen's face crinkled. 'About two miles north.' He looked pleased with himself.

'What?'

'Burnt-out Conestoga, bodies – a family.'

'So they're here?'

'Hereabouts for sure.'

Julah congratulated the Agency on the choice of guide. Bannen had turned up trumps alright. He'd known others spend weeks without a sniff, now, on only the third day, they'd struck gold. They'd been planning this for a while. As someone with Native American blood in his veins, Julah had a vested interest.

Michael looked out over the Reservation, taking in the tumbled heaps of trash and dilapidated shanties. Disheveled figures stumbled about, lay slumped on porches or by the dirt road: the sad remains of a once-proud Nation.

'Second class education, no jobs on the Reservation, and no-one would give them a job outside,' Michael had said to his brother-in-law. 'I've been going there for four years, and I'm just beginning to make some contact, get some trust.

Who can blame them? They are just one big problem nobody wants. Six-year-old kids on cocaine – I ask you!'

Julah and Bannen were riding north now, their horses loping easily over the rough terrain, eyes peeled for any movement. Bannen had promised him he'd found the perfect place, a small plain with a circle of sandstone bluffs: just the place for an ambush. Night was coming on fast. They camped, gathering some scrub to light a bright fire, banking it up sufficient for it to be sending a column of smoke into the dawn sky in a few hours. Perfect.

'The problem is they were actually too successful,' Michael said.

John looked surprised. 'I thought they just got whupped by the army and eradicated.'

'Not so.' Michael shook his head. 'They were a real barrier to the early exploration of the West. Probably held back colonization fifty years or more, too many of them.'

'What do you mean?'

'Well, funny thing is, if they had been less powerful, fewer, they would have survived better. We probably wouldn't have Reservations now and their descendants would be far better off, absorbed in society rather than quarantined.' Seeing John's puzzlement, Michael explained: 'Some guy at Stanford, Wazolski or Waslewski or something: I was reading his paper. He had a team build a social model, you know – large-scale thing – predictive.' Michael leaned across the table. 'It showed that if the Nations had been far smaller and less powerful, they would have had to be cooperative, therefore respected by the settlers, who in turn would have learned to depend on their goodwill, so both sides would have worked together, grown eventually into a merged community. The

USA would have been far more powerful than it ever has been, with a fifty year lead in exploration and prosperity, at least that's what the model predicts. Think of it – all the Edisons, the brightest immigrants from Europe and the world given a much bigger head-start. If only …'

Dawn was breaking. Julah shifted his head on the makeshift pillow. He had slept well. He raised his eyes to the blue, blue sky. A thin column of smoke rose high above. Good. Bannen had stayed awake. He was also keeping very still. There was no need, Julah thought. They would know if anything made a move. The slightest movement, the glint of sharpened stone in the rays of the rising sun, caught his eye. Way up on the bluff. Coming down soon. Good.

'It all started with Weslawski.' The Agent stared fixedly at Julah over the desk.

'The Stanford guy?'

'Yes. His ideas became prevalent a hundred years after his time, just when someone put the technology together to do something about it.'

'And they're actually thinking about …?'

'Yes. Top secret. Wouldn't want the Asians or the Chinese to get to know.'

'Surely they have it too?'

'Probably.'

'Then we could be fighting a war here, a war way back in our own history?' Julah pondered on the prospect. It was so complex he couldn't even guess at the consequences. Instead he focused on the one thing he could grasp. 'So the blood of the Nations will become part of the USA's success story. We will be strong – even stronger. And if we do it first …'

'Exactly. If it works out right, they won't have the technology or the power, the US will still be ruling the world.'

'Why me?'

'You're one of the few people trained for physical action. A warrior, if you like.'

'A rare profession now.'

'Yes. We need someone with the power of independent thought, and the training to implement it.'

'But I know nothing about the terrain, any of the things that went on.'

'You'll have a guide. He knows the place inside out.' In answer to Julah's unspoken question he added, 'He's not a warrior. He can't do it.'

The sun was way up now. Julah could imagine what could be seen from high on the bluff: a whole tempting encampment of settlers, ready to loot. That's all the hot-headed braves knew. The wiser heads never got a say. But they would, they would. When only the elders of the tribe and the women and children were left, sanity would return. Julah checked the power pack on the projector: fine. They were moving now, coming down for the kill. He waited.

The screaming warriors of the proud and powerful Nation encircled the mass of settlers and the soldiers covering them with rifles. They would have them as well, the rifles. The war whoops were designed to cow an enemy, to dominate. If any of them had looked closer, the patterns of repetitive movement of the figures behind the circle of wagons would have struck a false note. But none did. Their blood was up, now was the time.

Julah snapped on the protective screen. He and Bannen were within its field, together with the horses.

Then he raised his head, hawk nose against the blue sky, his lined face strained. With a tear in his eye, his hand moved on the control, slowly, deliberately. 'For the Nations!' he intoned, as the flickering blue wave licked out in an expanding circle, finally fading at the foot of the bluffs.

'Is that it?' Bannen asked.

'That's it.' Julah flicked off the screen, moved over to the projector and switched off the noise and bustle of the settler encampment. The air was still. No settlers, no soldiers, no war-whoops. No braves.

'Really? It's that simple?'

'God, I hope so.' Julah's voice was strained, choking. 'I hope so.'

Better die with honor than live in failure his great-grandfather had told him.

'What next?'

'We go back to the pick-up point, and a medical team goes in later to inoculate the tribe. There's a new generation coming. Come on.' Julah wheeled his mount and set off, wondering what the future would bring.

Soul Saver

One of Posy's

Sometimes in danger, I admit,
my soul has fluttered close to searing fire.
The flames of evil, malice, sin,
could singe my wings
before I came home safe.

And you, with honeyed words that lip-drip,
coo, cajole,
seduce me – you catch my soul
on golden thread, nets woven
to cocoon and wrap.

I do concede I am now safe,
hid from harm, under your care, your guard.
My soul can never flee,
no longer free:
trapped in your jar.

Dagmar Feels Appreciated

Another small person …

She's really happy these days. Billy's got a dark-green BMW and every Friday he takes her down the club in it. He doesn't want her to go in because the language is so bad, but when he's finished his game, he brings her out a drink and some crisps. She watches the car for him. It's a rough area.

He's good to her at home as well. He brings her stuff back from work – samples, he says.

Each Saturday he takes Dagmar shopping. They spend time together, checking the list she's made, with Billy adding up the prices. He's very careful, and she loves it when he helps her, finding a special offer or a cheaper brand. And he always pays in cash. Sometimes he seems to have a lot of it, a big wad of notes. When she asked him, he'd said, 'overtime, doll', but she doesn't know when he does it.

He doesn't like her to go out. He's kind that way. 'It's a bad neighbourhood.' He buys what she wants and brings it back at night. He doesn't always get everything she wants, or the right brand, but he says some things are bad for her or she needs to cut down, like her favourite mints and those little chocolate bars. She feels good that someone cares so much about her.

Dagmar doesn't always like it in bed, especially when he's been out late. He can be a bit rough. He's explained to her that that's the way it's done, so she supposes that must be true – but it's not how they show it on the TV. She'd been hoping they could have children, but he says it's too soon, it would spoil their lives at the moment. It's probably true, they have a good life.

She's been lonely since her mum died, well, in the daytime. Her mum had used to come to see her for a chat. She'd not been nice about Billy though, and a few months before she died, they'd had a row. Dagmar thinks it was the illness made her mum say those things, she wished she'd known about it, she would have forgiven her. Her sister won't speak to her now. She liked to phone her but they don't have a phone now. Billy says you don't need one any more if you have a mobile phone. But when he's out she can't use it anyway, so she doesn't really agree. But she knows he means well.

Sometimes he takes her out for the day, to the seaside or somewhere. That's lovely. He's had to go away, for weeks sometimes. Something to do with work. He comes back lovely and brown. It's so difficult for him, arranging everything to get shopping delivered for her. There's not so many nice things, but then, there's only one of her. And it costs five pounds for each delivery – she must be worth it for him to pay the extra. Even if she went out, she hasn't got any money really, anyway.

Dagmar sits waiting for Billy to come in. The TV's on as usual, and his tea's by the microwave, ready for her to pop it in. She's had a sandwich. She's happy, really.

If

A rant about journalism, people who keep on even when the truth is known

If I turned every subject into something I could rant
about, my fame would spread both far and wide
with something I could chant about
to vapid heads, whose only thought was
feelings of the common sort,
who'd vie to read my latest hit
on someone who I'd call a 'shit'
and point out all their lifestyle lies
and shout and yell.
Yes, I'd commit,
no matter that the subject was
in truth a fairly useless twazz
whose exploits mostly innocent, were tinged with
something I could use.
So would I care?
No, Billy Bragg come on! We see,
how common man's most common tongue can frame the
scene of right and wrong to those of mistuned brain.
That's up to them.
And down to me.

Ants

Ants,
Are in my pants.
And so I take
A particular stance.
As on their way,
Perhaps they may,
Decide to stray,
Begin to play.
So I say, 'Hey!
Don't go there.'

Cars

I look upon your wonders, Lord,
Creator of young Henry Ford.
Who made his mark with motor cars.
You made his world and he made ours!

The Banjo of the Gods

I once contacted the author Larry Niven for approval to use an idea of his in a story. He was friendly and complimentary.

I've not contacted Kilgore Trout (Philip Jose Farmer under a pen name borrowed from Kurt Vonnegut) but I acknowledge I have borrowed the central character from his story 'Venus on the Half-Shell'. You may think that it sounds Douglas Adamsy (Hitchhiker's Guide) – indeed it does – because Kilgore's story was one of the two main sources from which Adams got many of his ideas, the other being Robert Sheckley's 'Dimension of Miracles'.

Simon Wagstaff, Space Wanderer, gazed curiously at the object. 'What the hell is it?' Dirk's whisper susurrated along the deserted white museum corridor. Before them was a magnificent sight: golden strings stretched from ivory pegs along an ebony fretboard with mother-of-pearl decoration to the round resonator's silver filigree surround and the smoothest, whitest vellum taut beneath the rosewood bridge. It was a banjo – what a banjo!

'The Banjo of the Gods,' a small sign read.

Earlier, Simon and Dirk had stood outside the vast, imposing building with its enormous sign: 'Museam of the Universe'.

'Those Ooozcans never learned to spell.' Simon shook his head.

'What are we here for?' Dirk moaned. 'I don't like museams.'

'Aaah!' Simon said portentously. A light came into his eye, his head rose. 'But here, in this god-forsaken corner of the universe, is something famous, precious and completely unique.' And so it was …

Simon itched to touch it – to play it. After looking up and down the corridor, he vaulted over the barrier and approached the crystal case in which the object of his desire lay. His hands went straight to the lid, which to his surprise lifted easily. In a trice, he had grabbed the instrument, swung one end over the barrier to Dirk, and vaulted back. Somewhere, an alarm sounded. Dirk clutched the heavy instrument. It felt cool, smooth – special. Simon snatched it from him, dropped cross-legged onto the basalt floor, positioned his fingers and began to pluck the strings. Music filled the air, entrancing. And in the music were words, words that spoke loud and clear to their minds:

Through the eons of time and the boundless diversity of the universe, I speak: I, The Banjo of the Gods, the instrument of the ætherial beings who once ruled the multiverse, I speak to you, Space Wanderer, and tell you that by taking me into your possession, you have accepted a challenge – a quest, a task …

Simon dropped the Banjo in shock, then picked it up again hurriedly and inspected it for damage. 'Did you hear that?' he asked Dirk, who gave an absent nod. Simon noticed he was staring at a point behind his left ear. Simon turned. A small biobot stood there looking distinctly displeased and tapping one heavy pedule noisily on the gleaming stone.

'There's always one,' the bot sighed.

'Er, sorry, it was open, I just wanted to …'

'I know.'

'It spoke …'

'I know.'

'Well …' Simon held the instrument out to the bot.

'No – take it. Off you go.' The bot made shooing gestures.

'You should have it locked up,' Simon muttered sullenly.

'It was. It always escapes.' A look flitted across the bot's face that Simon could not quite interpret.

There was a pause.

'See you in three months.' The bot turned and made off rapidly down the corridor. '… usually takes that long …'

They stood outside the building again. No one had stopped them, no-one had followed them. The enormous sign gave a small groan and slipped slightly downwards.

'Couldn't build very well, either,' Simon said idly.

'What are we going to do now?' Dirk asked.

'Dunno.'

The strings of the Banjo began to resonate softly then words began to fill their heads again …

Space Wanderer, you have a quest.

'Okay. What?'

A quest of vast significance, a momentous task, for which all the beings of the universe will thank you. Your name will be inscribed on the pillars of the Halls of the Gods, where I, the Banjo of the Gods, make music for the …

'Can it!' Simon had been conned by more universal beings and deities than he could remember. 'Just tell me.'

Well, I have to explain the significance, otherwise your task will seem trivial.

'Just tell me, huh?'

'Should you be speaking to it like that?' Dirk hissed.

'Trust me.' Simon looked confident. 'It takes more than a talking banjo to impress me.' There was a deep rumble of strings and a coruscating tumble of twanging notes. Simon realised the Banjo was both growling and laughing at the same time. He felt a small chill run up his spine. 'Er, please go on …'

Why, thank you … The Banjo spoke with exaggerated politeness … *As I was saying: What is the single most important factor in life? What oils the wheels of human society, makes pain bearable, makes existence tolerable?*

'Soft toilet tissue?' Dirk interrupted.

Simon gave him a look, and was surprised at the Banjo's next words.

Very close! Your friend is moderately intelligent, Space Wanderer. Let us see if you can approach his excellent attempt.

Dirk preened, smirking annoyingly.

Despite himself, Simon made some suggestions. All were received with a tolerant *mmm* or an *oh!*

Eventually the Banjo appeared to lose patience.

Enough! I'll have to tell you. It is …

Simon made one last try. 'Political Correctness,' he blurted out. The Banjo hardly faltered.

… alcoholic drinks.

Simon felt as if a great light had suddenly shone. His eyes cleared, his brain de-fogged itself, and he saw the truth. 'Yes! So what's the problem? We got loads of it – anyone can make the stuff.'

Yes, but what you don't understand is …

'I used to make slow gin,' Dirk mused.

'What, with sloes?'

'No,' Dirk sounded impatient, *slow* gin. It slowed your perception of time, made things last longer. It was great stuff if you were going to …'

Ahem! If I may continue?

The two fell silent.

Alcohol is made by the action of what you call 'yeasts'.

'Yup – enzymes.' Simon looked to Dirk for approval.

Shut up and listen! The Banjo riffled up and down the

scale in displeasure, twanging ominously. *You may call them so, but in fact they are the product of pan-dimensional beings of vast intellect and achievement.*

'That's clever!' Simon could not be quiet for long. 'Do they have factories or farms or something?'

To his surprise, the Banjo sounded faintly embarrassed. *Er, no, not really. It's a sort of natural by-product.* The Banjo hesitated.

'But it's good of them to ship it all over the universe so us sentient beings can make alcohol …' Dirk smacked his lips, '… talking of which …' He gazed around, looking for something.

This time the Banjo sounded even more embarrassed. *Er, the distribution is not so much a favour to you, as a …*

Simon looked up, surprised at the Banjo's reticence. 'C'mon, spit it out!'

Okay, you asked for it. It's … um … more of a 'waste disposal' problem for them.

'You mean it's just their old rubbish? How strange.'

No.

'Not …' Simon began to contemplate the uncontemplatable. 'No!'

Yes. It's their sewage – faeces, if you want a nicer word than the one you are thinking at the moment. They are a very clean and proper race. They abhor mess and dirt, so early in their history they invented a machine that disposed of anything remotely messy by scattering it evenly throughout the universe and dimensions – the whole multiverse in fact.

'But …'

Yes, I know normally that would result in an almost zero, infinitesimal effect at any one place. The problem was, due to the influence of a chronosynclastic infundibulum in a nearby galaxy, the waste congregates on planets with habitable atmospheres, which is enough to create a sizeable quantity of 'yeast' on each planet.

'Yeuch!' Simon scowled, but then brightened up. 'Well, what you don't see can't hurt you. But as we've got yeast now, and it multiplies … what's the problem?'

It's like this. The 'yeast' has a half-life – which is passed on to its descendents genetically. Eventually all the offspring of one parent die off.

'So we've got to have a constant supply of it or it'll run out and …'

No alcoholic drinks … No inspirations, more mental breakdowns, more wars, practically the collapse of all sensible societies.

'What's their problem?' Simon was puzzled.

Well, they've found out about it descending in quantity on sentient beings and are completely shocked and embarrassed … They're going to stop the machine, even at the cost of destroying their own society, unless we find some way of persuading them.

Simon jumped up. 'Okay! I'm in! What do I have to do? Let's go!' He had always been a decisive Space Wanderer.

'So,' Simon Wagstaff, Space Wanderer, asked the Banjo, 'What must I do?'

The strings of the Banjo resonated and a deep, thrumming tone spoke out portentously: *First, we must undertake a long, wearisome journey, following the spaceways throughout the deepest depths of the Galaxy.*

'Really?' Simon felt important. 'Then what?'

Well, eventually you must convince the Council of Ptahhhs.

'What?' Simon was puzzled.

The High Council of the supreme, pan-dimensional beings whose machine spreads yeast through the Universe – remember, I told you about them?

'Okay, Okay, but you didn't tell me what they were called,

Okay?'

Er, Okay.

Simon didn't know whether the Banjo was mocking him or not. 'Carry on,' he snapped.

Oh, thank you indeed, sir, the Banjo said. *I've told you about the task. But first, we have a long, wearisome journey …*

Simon sighed. Dirk looked puzzled.

After a long, wearisome journey, the intrepid trio arrived at some godforsaken planet in some godforsaken galaxy in some godforsaken corner of the universe. *Here we are!* the Banjo exclaimed in ringing notes. Simon could have sworn he detected excitement in its tone.

'Where?' He was exhausted from the long, wearisome journey. Dirk was asleep.

Look! In front of them was a vast sign, strung across two mountain peaks. So enormous was the sign that the shade it created had wiped out at least ten thousand creatures which had lived, or tried to live, in its shadow. Simon squinted, and read the words aloud. 'Galactic Hootenanny, all welcome! What does that mean?' he asked.

Dirk said nothing. The Banjo said nothing, for a while … Then, after it judged that Simon's attention span had run out, the Banjo declared enthusiastically: *Hootenanny! Let's go!*

So they did.

During the month-long wearisome journey, Simon had played the Banjo often. They were close, he felt. He had picked some old bluegrass, strummed some minstrel ballads, flailed some folk songs, trailing his thumb over the drone fifth string. In short, they had had fun together, communed, experienced pleasure. Simon had so often gripped and caressed the Banjo, stroking the fretboard, grasping the silver filigree absently. The Banjo sat in his lap, intimately. They were one, united.

The Hootenanny was horrendous. Simon was shocked and hurt. As soon as they got there, the Banjo had left him, passing itself from hand to hand. Wantonly, the Banjo allowed itself to be strummed, stroked, picked, flailed and finally plucked enthusiastically in a far corner by all and sundry. Simon was embarrassed, lowering his head at the shame, pretending he didn't care, but he felt abused. Why had it not told him? Why had it deceived him?

Simon left the Hootenanny and wandered, as Space Wanderers are wont to do. Sat beneath a peculiar tree that dropped small fruits on his head that squeaked 'eat me', he bemoaned his fate. And ate them. What Simon did not know was that the fruit seeded itself by means of the digestive system of its host. What it did was to encourage random discharges which resulted in widespread seed–sites, with each seed surrounded by a rich, fertile deposit. After three days travail, Simon found a hostelry and time to recover. Where was the Banjo? Where was Dirk? he wondered. He soon found out.

Come!

Simon shook himself awake. He felt tired, but better. He checked his body gradually, finding most things in working order, to his relief. He looked up. Dirk stood there, holding the Banjo. It was a sorry sight. Its fretboard was grimy with grease and bits of pork scratchings, the previously pristine vellum was stained and dirty, its silver was tarnished with wine-stains. Simon was totally disgusted.

We've got work to do, the Banjo declared ringingly. *Remember the Ptahhhs?*

Simon was not impressed. 'Well, *I* do. Do you? You've been off gallivanting, enjoying yourself with god knows who, in god knows what ways, and you dare come back and ask me? You are despicable – and filthy, soiled,' he added.

The Banjo of the Gods was nothing if not tactful and sympathetic. It had dealt with famous figures of history, deities, heroes and demons. Using the full power of its experience and understanding, the Banjo spoke: *Shut up! Get up! And get to work … Now!* Then it added, *Clean me up, Dirk. I need a polish.*

Simon worked hard on the speech. He applied every ounce of his intelligence to a cogent and coherent argument. He used emotion, sympathy, logic, sophistry, Pythagorasy, ellipsis, emolumental deracination, and all kinds of other techniques he, as a Space Wanderer, had found, discovered and learnt across the wide universe, the galaxies and civilisations. He spared no detail, no corner of logic, rehearsing in front of Dirk: declaiming, gesticulating, emoting, pleading, commanding, imploring conceding, repeating, conceiting, pressing home, allowing, insisting, contradicting, rescinding, long-winding, concluding …

'Perfect,' breathed Dirk.

'Perfect!' Simon shouted.

Okay! Time to go home. We've all had our fun.

Simon looked up in amazement. Dirk had brought the Banjo back. It was pristine, vellum scrubbed clean of the grimy fingerings of the multitude. Its golden strings vibrated in the light, pure and gleaming. Yet Simon knew how tarnished it was. As it had been passed from hand-to-hand, shameless and wanton at the Galactic Hootenanny, he had lost his respect for it forever. But one thing puzzled him.

'Er, what about the Council of Ptahhhs?'

Done and dusted. All decided.

'But I haven't given my speech, pleaded my case.'

Oh, that? Don't worry, they eavesdropped.

'What?'

They listened in to your rehearsals. They ARE pan-dimensional beings, you know.

'So they understood, accepted my words. I saved the Universe?'

Well … The Banjo sounded unduly reticent.

'Well what?'

Er … The Banjo seemed at a loss. *Did you ever hear about ginger?*

'What the hell are you talking about?' Simon was annoyed. 'What the hell is ginger?'

Well, on the planet Earth …

'I'm from Earth,' Simon interrupted.

… a long time ago, continued the Banjo, *people used 'ginger' for cooking. It appeared to be the root of a plant. I say 'appeared to be' because in truth, ginger roots were actually the toenails of a race of pan-dimensional beings, materialised into the specific location of Earth and its inhabitants. For many years, the relationship was mutually beneficial. Many people benefited from flavoursome dishes, and the pan-dimensional beings benefited from regular pedicures. What could be better?*

'Well, I've never heard of this "ginger",' Simon interrupted.

That's because, before your birth, the people of Earth had already contacted other space-going races, and learned of the pan-dimensional beings.

'So?' Simon was belligerent. He was wondering about the Council of Ptahhhs and trying to work out if this had anything to do with anything.

Er, I guess the bottom line is – would you be happy if you knew you were grating some pan-dimensional being's toenails into your food?

Simon saw the point. 'Yeuch!' he exclaimed.

Exactly, said the Banjo.

'So what happened?'

Well, of course everyone stopped using ginger.

'That's no problem – I never missed it.'

Typical selfish human behaviour, the Banjo sounded censorious. *Do you know what happened? Do you care? I'll tell you* … Simon could tell the Banjo was angry. Dirk flashed him a warning look, but kept his grip on it. *Thanks to the crude whims of the people of your planet, a whole pan-dimensional race, who had done nothing but good, had uplifted many species and races, tumbled into decline and despair* …

Simon, sensing something bad, decided to take a conciliatory tone. 'Well, I'll try it if that helps.'

What?

'Er, ganger – ginger, I mean.'

The thrum of the bass string was prevalent in the Banjo's tone. The vellum was at full stretch. Simon recognised that the Banjo was exceedingly impatient. *Too late!* the Banjo twanged solemnly. *Devoid of pedicures, with no alternative, these poor beings hobbled around, becoming victims of stumbling incidents and a complete loss of confidence, hiding and retreating, until their civilisation crumbled, and one by one, they hobbled to their end.*

'Bloody sad!' Dirk intoned.

Bloody sad indeed.

Simon's attention focused. This 'ginger' story was all well and good, but why was the Banjo recounting it now? His brain worked slowly but surely. Ahah!

'Yes. But how did the Council of Ptahhhs receive my argument. Did they concede in the face of its unarguable logic?' Simon needed to know – it was a 'pride thing'.

Er … the Banjo sounded reluctant.

'Spit it out!' Simon commanded. 'You know you've got to tell the truth.'

How did you know that? Well, they decided, from your speech, with you being a representative of all the sentient species in the universe, after description of your life, your feelings, sentiments, moral code, the quality of your argument and your logic, that they were convinced.

… *Hooray!* the Banjo added weakly.

Simon had to know. 'What?' He demanded. 'What convinced them?'

It all came in a rush: *They had thought that they were dropping crap on beings who were sentient, caring, with the same moral values and fastidious nature as themselves.*

'Which they wouldn't do?'

Ooh, no! Never!

'So what happened. Come on.'

The Banjo's twang was quiet and reluctant. *On the basis of your speech, they decided that the other species of the universe are sub-sentient, crude, coarse, with little or no moral values, godless sinners … er, who deserve to be crapped on in abundance. Apparently the only species they respect are seagulls and pigeons …*

'Enough!' Simon was angry. He did not even know if the Banjo's story was true. 'We go back.'

It had been a long, wearisome journey. Simon and Dirk stood outside the vast building with its wonky sign: 'Museam of the Universe'. The bot appeared at the top of the steps. 'We're back then?' It said cheerily.

Simon took the Banjo, which had not spoken for a month, from Dirk and thrust it into the bot's arms. The bot took it with a grin. 'Let me guess …' Simon looked sullen. 'You made a long, wearisome journey …' It wasn't really a question. 'You went to a Galactic Hootenanny.' Simon's eyes widened, but he still said nothing. 'You saved the universe.' Simon grimaced, he was beginning to feel used. 'And you are *very* unhappy about the whole thing.' The bot's voice softened. 'Here. Come in, and I'll pour you both a glass of Tyrrhian Panther-Sweat.'

Simon's face brightened. Dirk grinned.

The bot placed the Banjo back in its case. This was a new one, with big locks and complicated code-wheels. 'He'll still get out, I just know it. He always does …' he sighed.

Simon looked at the bot. 'You mean?'

'Every time. He just loves Hootennanies.'

A single, plangent stopped-chord sounded, a seventh with one string bent into a bluesy, questioning note. It was majestic, heart-tugging, and final.

'Let's get that drink,' Simon said.

He took one last look at the glistening banjo, then turned to the bot and asked, 'Is he really The Banjo of the Gods?'

The bot frowned, leaned forward, peering.

'That's what it says on the label.'

Vintage

(Posy)

In last year's vintage,
I savoured fruit in spring and sun in summer.
By autumn it was soured,
and clogged the palate
– was undistinguished.

Surfeit drove the hazy days
and slumb'rous nights:
with senses dulled,
no will to strive,
no mind to care.

Where once I supped on mother's milk
– *soft ways*
of warmth: belonging,
growing, changing, living –
now all I have is this:

> Sour and aging;
> last year's vintage.
>
> All that's left …
> a deep-red glass
> of bitter bile.

Cabin

I had in mind, much as in 'The Presence of Jalendu', what the absence of something might imply, or in this case what is unsaid, despite protestation. For some reason, Br'er Rabbit and the briar patch sprang to mind.

Today was a good day. We went fishing and I got two fat trout for Mac and me. The other two won't be eating. The days here are fine, no problems – it's just the nights. It's getting dark now and I'm sitting at the table in the cabin. The fish are in front of me, on a plate. I was going to gut them. Night is when it gets difficult.

It was Mac's idea to come up here for a week or two. Walt and Jem jumped at the idea – time away from our wives, a chance to hunt, fish, have a good time; to spin a few yarns and drink some beer.

I could get in the truck any time and drive away, there's nothing to stop me; nothing to stop any of us. There never was. The truck is Mac's – bright red, she's a beauty: six-up cab and plenty of room in the back. It's not far to Teller, on the back trail. I'd be there in an hour or so.

It's getting cold. I could get some wood from the shed. There's no reason why I can't go out there. Jem's in the shed right now. Don't know where his dog's got to …

I took Mac out on the lake to fish, that's how I got the trout. We found Walt there, so he came back with us – he's out by the tree now.

I can't see anything outside the window. The sun's gone

down but I can still see the trees. There's nothing, no one.

I thought Mac was gonna make it. He's sat here, next to me. He looks cheerful, but it's not real. He doesn't speak.

I wonder how Nell's getting on. Maybe she's worried about me. We were supposed to phone from Teller Tuesday, but Mac didn't feel like going and neither did I. Come to think of it they must be worried by now. I could go phone her tomorrow, I guess. I can take the truck anytime, Mac won't mind.

We started out eight days ago, singing, cracking jokes, like kids let out of school. It's a fair haul up here, so Mac and I spelled each other, changing over at the rest stops. We took a full day to get to Fairview, where we stopped for the night. It was a nice town: good food, comfortable beds and a lively bar – what more could a bunch of men away from their wives want?

So next day we were in good spirits, the sun was out and the highway clear. We'd stopped in the last town before the turn-off for a bite. None of us had been in these parts before, so we talked to the guy in the diner there. Funny guy, Native American, weird accent. He was friendly at first, but when we told him the name of the place we were heading for, he stepped back and started ranting at us. Maybe the cabin owner had cheated him or something. He wasn't aggressive, but it was pretty weird. But hey! We got here okay.

The cabin's good: three bedrooms, big main room, usual stuff; a small lean-to shed outside with plenty of wood stacked ready for the nights. It's set by a lake, just like in a movie, with forest around, mountains behind. As the truck growled up the steep trail, we all gave a yell as we rounded a bend and the cabin came into view. We'd seen pictures, but the reality was better. Hound was barking his head off.

We'd been lucky. Most decent cabins were taken this

time of the season, and we'd decided on the break at short notice. It was Mac's brother who found it. Some guy in his shop was moaning how he'd rented his new cabin to someone who'd skipped without paying after just a few days. We did find a few personal things lying around which we packed up in case the previous renter came back.

That first night we were cheerful. We cooked steaks on the barbecue and drank a few beers. After a while, though, Walt got fidgety and decided he'd go in. Jem soon followed with the dog. Mac and I joked about it – the night was warm – no bugs about, so we assumed the other guys were just tired. Mac and I sat up yarning until it was really dark. Suddenly, I got this weird feeling. Can't say exactly what it was, I guess it might have been the night chill or something. Mac agreed pretty quickly when I suggested making a move so we doused the fire and carried the remaining beers in. I noticed Mac looking over his shoulder, and joshed him about it. After that, it was sort of quiet. The four of us sat round the big room, not saying much. None of us slept well and the dog was whining all night. Mac and I bunked in the big bedroom and he was turning over most of the time. I assumed it was the long journey.

Next day we were out early, full of the country around us, glad we'd come. I wrote off the restless night and looked forward to more days like it. Hound was off in the woods.

The second night, it was much worse. We'd been calling for Hound. Damn dog just lit out, took off up the mountain somewhere, howling. We heard his yelps for a while in the distance, then there was silence. Jem was a tad upset, he'd got the dog from his wife's brother, and it was a well-trained dog. We promised to help him search the next day. At first he was pretty reluctant to come back. Until it started to get dark.

I laughed at Walt when he locked the door, asked him

who he thought was going to visit us up here – the previous inhabitant? But truth be told, I felt more comfortable myself. I didn't know what had gotten into me – or the others. On the way up we'd talked about some night hunting. No one mentioned it now and I was grateful.

Each night it got worse. No one spoke about it, but I could see it in their faces. We couldn't find any trace of the dog, and Jem was pretty depressed. We were supposed to go down the store for more supplies on the Thursday, but no one could be bothered. We didn't talk about it. We did some hunting, but there was always that thought at the back of my mind: that night would inevitably come.

Jem was first. He went out to fetch some wood and didn't come back. He's still out there, under the big roof beam. The next day, it was Walt. Mac hung on two more days. We got quite excited about the fish today, until Walt turned up and we had to bring him back. I think that's what finally got to Mac. He kept telling me we could leave anytime we liked. I know that. Of course we could. The truck's there if we want it. We can go or stay as we choose.

Tonight, we'd sat down at the table together, inside. After we'd locked the door. I was going to gut the fish. That was a while ago. It's dark now. I don't want to light the lamp, it's in the window.

Mac's here. He looks as if he's smiling, but he isn't. The gun did that. It's still in his hand.

There's nothing outside. I can leave anytime I want, I know that. I can go out and take the truck. Mac won't mind. I'll set here a while longer. Perhaps I'll gut the fish. The knife's in my hand, ready.

Greyland

Ice lying on the lake,
And frost upon the bough
Snow-smitten heathen land!
There's little here enow[1]

Crake sounding on the air
The picking's poor they call
Our stone-enmounded hof [2]
Will not see joy in hall

Invected[3] icy ground
Step-slipping our foray
And each new hidden place
Engrails[4] our current prey

---

[1] Archaic version of 'enough'
[2] 'hof' – hall/house
[3] 'invected' heraldic pattern like little arches – ruts
[4] 'engrails' again heraldry – a pattern of cups/grails – infers hiding

Green Magic

In woody boughs and willow canes the green blood flows

and drives the life of shoots and leaves in different ways.

There's mystery and likewise threat within their springing growth:

the lashing bramble, weedy root and tangling vine invade

to creep within the dark of night. Red-blooded life must wary be,

for mingling green and red can lead to tragedy.

Gabriel Coore

This is multi layered, to say the least. Pay attention!

Gabriel Coore leaned forward, running his hands over the smooth, metallic object which lay in his lap. A complex shape, it was silvery with no sign of corrosion or any markings or joins he could discern apart from a cylindrical projection. Little did Gabriel know that this object would bring more trouble to his life than anything he'd ever known before, and ten years in the future he would rue the day…

Damn! He was doing it again. He put a line through the last sentence. When would he get this writing lark right? He just kept forgetting.

There was a knock. Gabriel started with surprise. A visitor at this hour? He put the object into the sideboard cupboard, calling out, 'Coming'.

He opened the door and on the step stood a small, round man. He had something wrong with him, but Gabriel could not quite identify what. 'Yes?' he enquired.

'You have my property,' the man stated in a curious, flat tone.

'I'm sorry?'

'You have something of mine, a metal object. You found it on the beach.'

Gabriel thought quickly. 'Sir, I am a writer and an artist. While it is true I may sometimes collect driftwood and other objects for my pieces, I am not a treasure hunter, nor do I carry a metal detector.'

The man did not respond. His face remained blank.

'Is that all?' Gabriel began to close the door.

'Such was my information.'

'Then your information was wrong.' Gabriel wondered how the man knew.

'Logically, you are the most likely ….'

'"Likely" does not mean certainty. I am sorry, but I know nothing of any old bits of metal you may have lost.'

'You don't understand. This is most important.'

'I'm sure it is, and I hope you find it. Goodnight.' Gabriel closed the door. From behind the curtains, he observed the man hesitate, then begin wandering along the road.

Yes, that'll do it. Mysterious object, mysterious stranger. Good! Okay, what next? Ah yes … The pen scribbled across the page.

Gabriel stared after the figure of the man as it disappeared into the distance down the sandy beach road. He retrieved the object from the cupboard and looked at it more closely. He ran his fingers over the smooth metal, feeling for any kind of distortion on the surface. None was apparent. What did it do? What was it for? Why was it so important to his unwelcome visitor?

Right, that would do for starters. Tomorrow, he'd reveal a few things to tantalise and then go for the denouement. This was shaping up well! He opened the desk drawer to put the notebook away, and saw the metal thing. Once again he picked it up. It seemed as if a small knob was projecting from it. Had it been there before? He pulled at it and found he could twist it.

He sat in an armchair in a room which, in his mind, was familiar. Why, it was all here, exactly as he had described it. With a sense of foreboding, he went to the window and stared out. Outside was a beach, and a sandy road leading away. Some way down it, a small figure stood, silhouetted against the evening sky, not moving.

He stepped back, twisting the knob the opposite way.

He dropped the thing back in the desk drawer and slammed it shut. Gazing around at his study, he breathed a sigh of relief. What kind of vision had that been? Shaking his head, he left the cottage and walked down the village street towards the pub. A few pints and a steak and kidney pie and he'd be right as rain. The story would be finished tomorrow.

'Evening!' a cheery voice called as he entered the low-beamed parlour. A wood fire flickered in the grate, and there was a buzz of conversation. Jack was already pulling his pint as he came up to the bar.

'Evening, Jack. Good to see you.'

Jack looked at him in amusement. 'Why do you say that? You see me most nights.'

'Oh, just I've been writing and a few funny thoughts came into my head. It's nice to get out in the fresh air and come down here.'

Jack placed the pint pot in front of him. 'Well, all that sitting about does you no good, I keep telling you. Pie tonight?'

'Yes please.' He nodded to an empty corner.

Just as he was halfway across the floor, Jack called out, 'Oh, I forgot. There was a feller here looking for you.'

'Who?'

'Dunno, some little fellow, fat. Funny-looking, flat voice, you know, expressionless.'

'What did he say?'

'Just asked for the writer. Well, there's only you round here.'

'Yes. Did you …'

'Yep, did he find you?'

'No.'

'Oh. Said he needed to talk, urgent. Expect he'll come back later. Funny bloke.'

The man was still there. Had he been there all night? Gabriel Coore turned from the window and wondered what he should do. He went to the sideboard and took the metal thing out of the cupboard. He noticed that the projecting knob was a darker shade, gripped it and twisted it.

The cottage was quiet. The morning sun streamed into the room. The whole place was unfamiliar. What had happened? He got up from the writing desk and went to the window. Outside was a village street, busy with passing people and traffic. Down the road, he could see a picturesque thatched pub. Gabriel heard a noise in the room above and at once made for the door, sliding the bolt back silently and closing it gently as he left.

'Scotch, please. Double!' he barked at the man behind the bar.

'Certainly sir. New here?'

'Er, yes.'

'Thought I hadn't seen you before. Name's Jack, I'm the landlord.' Jack looked expectant as he placed the drink in front of him.

'Er, Gabriel, Gabriel Coore.' Gabriel downed the scotch in one and signalled for another.

Jack took the glass and hesitated.

'Just had a terrible shock,' Gabriel told him.

As Jack brought the whisky back, Gabriel noticed his gaze.

'What's that metal thing? It's weird.'

'Er, I don't know, I found it on the beach.'

'Whereabouts?'

'Just over …' Gabriel became aware he didn't even know if

there was a beach around here.

'Swanscombe?'

'Er, yes.' Gabriel took a sip of the whisky.

'Funny, cos there was someone here yesterday askin' about a metal thing.'

'What?'

'Well, he came to find a local chap, writer. Lives in that cottage up the street, you know.'

Gabriel gulped the whisky and pushed the glass forward.

'You sure sir? Another? It must have been one hell of a shock.'

Gabriel nodded. 'So, this man. What happened?'

Jack turned from the optic as he filled the glass. 'Well, I told the writer chap about him, right? He was a small man, round and fat. Sort of funny-lookin', can't quite put my finger on it. Asked about the writer, then about this metal thing.' He placed the glass in front of Gabriel. 'I remember now, I forgot to tell the chap that bit. He seemed upset and it drove it from my head.'

Gabriel did not know what to think. After paying the landlord, he retired to a corner, nursing his drink. What should he do? There was only one thing to do. He lifted the metal object and twisted the knob.

He took his coffee to the writing desk and sat, pulling out the notebook from the drawer, noticing the metal object as he did so. A shiver of anxiety passed through him and he glanced down the corridor at the front door. Immediately, he was up and shooting the bolt across. He'd forgotten to lock up last night – how could he have done that? He'd only had two pints with his pie.

Trying to keep calm, he sat again and took a slug of coffee – hot and strong, just as he liked it. He brightened up. He decided he'd been dreaming or something. He shook his head and began to write.

Gabriel stood on the beach road, staring towards his house. It sat, familiar as ever with the sand lapping round it and his collections of silver driftwood stacked to one side. He turned, but there was no-one else on the road. For one moment, he'd thought …

He hurried towards the house.

A knock came at the door. Irritated, he put down his pen and went to open it.

On the threshold stood a small man. A round man. A strange-looking man. A flat, expressionless voice broke the silence.

'You have something of mine. A metal object.'

'I've no idea what you are talking about. I hear you've been asking for me in the pub. You're obviously unbalanced, so please go away or I shall call the police.'

'Police? No police.' The little man stepped back. 'It must be returned, one way or another.'

'I've told you.'

'I know. I *know*.' He stood in silence for a while. 'Very well, I shall return with someone to take it, I am sorry. His presence will damage you, but the object must be returned. I hope you understand.' He turned and was gone.

Gabriel sat in fear. The whisky wasn't helping now, in fact it was making things worse. He felt blurred, unreal. Every now and then he would lurch to the window and look down the beach road. Eventually, on the umpteenth time of looking, there was something there. Something or somebody? With his alcohol-blurred vision, he could see the little man, but there was something large and indistinct behind him, like a dark cloud … as it came closer, he could not believe what he saw. He rushed for the sideboard, sobbing, stumbling over the footstool by the armchair, crashing headlong into the solid wood. He could hear a heavy tread on the road outside, getting louder. He wrenched the cupboard door open and pulled out the metal thing. He'd go back, that was it – go where he'd be safe.

He sat back. This was going well. All that silly nonsense with the metal thing and the loony had driven him to new heights of creativity. He'd thought he'd been getting obsessed when he'd had that dream, but no, it was ideal story-fodder.

He got up and headed for the kitchen. Another cup of coffee and it would be finished. He couldn't wait.

'Morning, Jack.'

'Oh, hello. Feeling better today?'

'Yes, I was a bit down last night, wasn't I?'

'That little bloke, did he …?'

'Yes, and I'd be obliged if you didn't tell strangers where I live in future.'

'Oh, he was a nuisance?'

'Yes, a loony.' He took his pint. 'But he did give me a cracking finish to my latest story, I'm really pleased with it.'

'Good. But I forgot to tell you about the metal thing.'

'Don't worry, he went on about that.'

'Yeah, but there was a bloke in here this morning with a metal thingy – how's that for a coincidence?'

'What?' He put down his pint on the bar and stared at Jack. 'What was it like?'

'Well, a kinda twisty shiny thing, with a round bit sticking out.'

'Who was this man?'

'A stranger. Never seen him before. Wait … he told me his name. Coote, no, Coore.'

A cold feeling gripped him. 'Coore?'

'Yes, Gabriel Coore.'

'Quick, tell me, where did he go?'

'That's the funny part. He downed three double whiskies and sat in the corner fiddling with the thing. Next time I looked, he'd gone.'

'Christ! Jack, I've got to go.' His head was in a whirl, his only thought was to get home quickly and lock the doors. Gabriel Coore, here? With a metal thing? His dream last night? It was impossible.

Gabriel crouched by the writing desk, hoping to stay out of sight of the windows of the study. He heard the hammering on the door, the sound of splintering wood. The crashing sounds had his heart racing, and he desperately twisted the metal object, but his efforts were futile. He cried in frustration, dropping to his knees as heavy footsteps echoed down the hall.

He reached his house, panting with the unaccustomed effort. The door lay open, smashed. Fearfully, he stepped over the mess and peered into the hall. The doors were open and there was trail of broken objects, the small table and its china swan, the pictures from the walls tumbled to the floor. There was no sound, no movement. Hardly believing his own bravery, he followed the trail to his study. Nothing!

Quickly, he moved to the desk and pulled the drawer open. He felt relief as he saw the notebook safe in its place, then his eyes fixed on the metal object. If the loony had come back with some thugs, why hadn't they found the object? Why hadn't they waited for him? What had they really wanted? With trepidation, he checked the safe, his drawers of precious coin collections, his books. All intact.

He sat at his desk and took the metal object in his hands.

All this fuss over such a strange thing. Idly, he lifted it and twisted the knob.

The door was bulging as some mighty weight thrust against it. He crouched in the empty room as it gave way and he saw what lay behind it. He could not move. He desperately tried to turn the knob back, but it was futile. He held it out as the horror approached, while the little man stood, smiling, outside.

Footsteps

This is a personal 'Posy' favourite of mine

We turn towards those other hills,
The bare-backed man and I.
To make our way in solitude,
To take for once a winding route
Beneath a winding sky.

In those far hills we are alone,
My bare-backed man and I.
Kept warm at night in caves of stone,
No mind to chance the might of Rome.
Far from that place we lie.

We are not tempted to return,
Despite a welcome hearth,
For down that road our death awaits
And trying to escape our fates,
We press towards the north.

No foot will trace our path this morn,
Nor either other days.
The bare-backed man and I, forlorn,
From our beginnings neatly torn,
'Released,' he often says.

A soul is empty once it's lost
All hope and youth and joy.
Upon the tempest it is tossed,
In dreadful torment often crossed.
As pain and grief alloy.

We better live like this than die –
Some life is yet to reap.
But time draws on through curving ways,
And ever nearer loom the days,
When we will have to sleep.

Discovery

The chair on which he sat
An empty place with space around

The road that he once trod
Forgotten now. And then I found

The letter that he wrote
His tender words adorn the page

But not for me, alas.
For now, I'll sit. And then I'll rage.

The Book

A mystery, once again written in an old-fashioned style. I borrowed the idea of the book itself from a fellow-writer, Richard Hawkins. However the style and story are all mine.

It was with some trepidation that I approached the imposing grey stone building once more, its towering façade spiked here and there with turrets and towers. I gazed up at the engraved stone lintel above the carved double doors. *Ex domo ad ubi?* read the motto of the Deeves family, and indeed they had followed that motto for generations, producing adventurers and leaders who had shaped the Empire. I had been at school with Gerard Deeves, the current incumbent, but had not seen him for several years. As I recalled, the last time had been in India, where he'd been lambasting a boy in the market who it appeared had tried to cheat him. His larger-than-life figure with its shock of fair hair and florid complexion made him hard, if not impossible, to ignore. I chuckled to myself at the memory, but then my thoughts became more sober. What had brought me here today was no laughing matter, and I was fearful for the condition of my erstwhile companion.

The letter had come a week ago. Not the kind of letter I would expect from Gerard Deeves. It was sorrowful and hesitant, with none of the careless bonhomie so characteristic of the man. Of course, I had read of the affair of his fiancée. I did not know her, but I had penned my sympathies. Perhaps it was this that had caused him to request my visit, or perhaps he might have done so anyway. Whatever the spur that had driven him, I was here at Deeves Hall.

When the manservant showed me into the drawing room, I must confess I was shocked. The man that greeted me was hunched, hesitant and nervous. His voice faltered and paused. After a while he regained a little of his old spirit, and waving his hand around the room, began describing some of his collection. He had always been a great collector – objets d'art, books, talismans and relics – anything out of the ordinary, with a story to it, a mystery. It did not surprise me that he did not mention the reason I had come, his invitation, or, more accurately, his plea. Deeves retained the manners of an earlier generation, and despite my shock and concern for his welfare, I recognised and appreciated his conversation and his attempts to put me at my ease as he treated me as a welcome guest.

While Deeves had been busy with his mysteries, perversely I had gained somewhat of a reputation for debunking such matters. I had always preferred the scientific method above all religions or spiritual beliefs. In my investigations, I had never seen evidence of truly supernatural events. All my cases were either uncovered as rumour, hoax or mistake by one person or another, or were simply so vague as to remain obscure. It was this facet of my talents that Deeves had called upon, though I could not guess for what reason.

I retired to prepare for dinner. Remembering my visits as a youth, on my way up to my room it came upon me to take the opportunity to gaze once more into the magnificent library on the first floor, one which stretched across the whole front of the house. Not only was it one of the most imposing rooms I had ever, seen, but its collection of books was unparalleled and its sumptuous sofas were, in my youth, places to settle for hours, gratefully reading despite the entreaties of my friends to engage in more active pursuits. But to my surprise, the library door was firmly locked and it was with some little disappointment that I repaired to my room.

Dinner that evening was a gloomy affair. Although Deeves made an effort, it was clear that his earlier energies had drained him somewhat, and we suffered long pauses in conversation that were embarrassing. The food and the wine were excellent however, so it was with a comfortably replete feeling, as well as one of burning curiosity, that I settled in the study before a glowing, well-stoked fire.

Deeves sat back in the creaking leather armchair, brandy on one hand, cigar in the other, and began to speak. 'You may have heard of the problems surrounding my fiancée, Louisa.' His voice broke for a moment, then he resumed. 'They occurred in very mysterious circumstances.'

'But the newspapers said it was an illness.' Immediately I cursed myself for a tactless fool, but in truth it was surprise that drove the words from my lips. Deeves raised a hand. 'That's what they said, it is true. But then …' He paused to take a thoughtful puff at his cigar. '… they don't know it all.'

You can imagine how intrigued I became. What were the circumstances of the affair that had not been disclosed? How did it concern me?

The book was ancient, Deeves said. Yet it was written in plain English and was understandable. That was why he had purchased it, in some exotic bazaar in a country he'd visited – he'd even forgotten when. Deeves had never been a great reader. After his first inspection, he'd never opened it again, admiring it for its ancient cover and imposing designs.

'The damn johnny who sold it to me kept jabbering on about it, saying he was only selling it because he had to buy food for his family, that he should have burnt it. Can you imagine? Burning an ancient book, bound in gold? The man was crazy. Certainly crazy to tell me of his need, because I got it off him for a pretty good price, I'll tell you.' Some of my companion's spirit was showing again now, his words coming to life as he relived a moment from his youth. But a moment later, he was sombre again, his face drawn and pale.

'She started to read it. She always was a fanciful soul, imaginative, full of ideas and life – so full of life. A kinder, sweeter, person you could never have known.' He excused himself as he dabbed his eye and I felt a rush of affection and grief for him. After a pause, he began to speak again, steadily and, it seemed, with concentration and purpose. 'At first, she was full of excitement. She would recite to me some of the story. It was indeed a wonderful story as she told it. She would read for a short while after lunch, before our stroll through the park. Then things began to change.'

I leaned forward, heedless of my empty glass.

'She started to come here not see me but to read the book – I swear it,' he added, noticing my expression. 'She would come in, greet me with the barest of niceties, then beg my leave to venture upstairs to the library. I could refuse her nothing, but as the days went by, she changed. I noticed her face was drawn and there were dark circles under her eyes. She asked to borrow the book to take away and I made some excuse – I said it was because of the insurance. But in truth, I was gravely concerned – so concerned that I went behind her back and spoke to her father, asking his opinion of her condition and venturing my concerns. He admitted she had been 'a little quiet' and had spent much time closeted in her room. This he ascribed to her anticipation of our forthcoming nuptials, which were just a few months away. Privately, I felt no such motive could be valid as Louisa had hardly mentioned our wedding in the previous weeks. But I kept my own counsel.

She no longer spoke about the book. When I asked her about it, her face became troubled and she would avoid my gaze, passing her interest off as a need to see how the story ended, nothing more, and making light of the subject.

But the book was the cause of our first row. I had to go up to town for a few weeks to settle some business, and decided to let the staff have some time away, closing up the house in their absence. Louisa was furious when I told her and demanded possession of the book. It made me all the more steadfast in my refusal, and eventually she stormed out. How I rue that day! I was terribly upset, but I'd resolved that we could never start our life together if I were to give in to tantrums. However, at the same time I was deeply shocked, so before I left I asked our doctor to visit her on a pretext of a regular check and make sure she was all right – and …' Here he made a long pause, and began again with almost a whisper. '… God forgive me, not just physically.'

Realising what this implied, I felt sympathy for my friend. What would I do if ever I found myself in such a position: the one I loved behaving erratically, her family seemingly unnoticing? I tried to reassure myself that I should approach it with clear logic, but admitted all might be different in reality.

'I considered destroying the book, or at least removing it. Instead, I decided to see what the few weeks break might bring, to see it out despite the doubts and concerns that filled my head and tormented me while I tried to carry out my business in London.

'On my return, I was greeted by the worried face of Louisa's father at my carriage door. He begged, "Please, Gerard, come at once. We tried to contact you, but we did not know where you were staying and there was nobody here at the house to ask." It was true that in the dramatic moments prior to my leaving, in my concern and, I am ashamed to admit, in my anger, I had not given Louisa the information I had intended. I cursed myself as we sped to her side, whip cracking and the carriage rocking dangerously.

'She looked terribly ill, as if in some kind of fever. Her lips were moving, mouthing strange names, making incoherent pleas to unknown strangers, her eyeballs rolling behind the closed lids as if in a waking dream. The doctor motioned me outside.

'"She is talking about a book," he told me. My heart sank. "That damned book! I'll burn it now. Now, I tell you," I shouted at him. He looked me in the eyes and calmly told me that it might be the worst thing possible. The doctor explained that in his opinion – and he had had some training in the aspects of the behaviour of the human mind – Louisa had an obsession. For whatever reason, she had a driving urge to finish reading the book. Nothing else mattered. How she had got into this state he could not comprehend, but he assured me that destroying the book would abandon her to the condition which now controlled her, perhaps permanently. Better, he reasoned, to allow her to complete her obsessive task, then get her well and guard against it happening again. "There is no doubt her health is suffering. It is as if the life is being drawn out of her," he told me solemnly, his face dolorous.

'You can understand I was beside myself, torn. Should I allow this book, apparently the cause of my dear Louisa's despair and illness, back into her hands?'

I murmured my sympathies as best I could. I could not imagine the pain and suffering involved, the horror of such a situation. My God, what my friend had faced!

'And you did? Bring her the book?'

His head lowered. 'Yes. May God forgive me.'

'And …?'

'I was not present when she received the book. I brought it from the library and placed it in the hands of the doctor, who bore it immediately to Louisa's bedside. According to his account, she seized it immediately, showing every sign of animation, sitting up, eyes open, with all sign of illness fled.'

'All?'

'The doctor said she was pale, drawn, emaciated, but activated by some intense energy which filled her. He declared he had never seen anything like it.'

'And?'

Deeves's eyes were slits, his face unreadable. His brandy and cigar lay forgotten. His hands had formed fists, clenched and white. Slowly, his eyes opened wider and focussed on me, his mouth opened and he spoke.

'By all accounts she was as normal, sitting up in bed, reading the book, calling for a glass of lemon tea and some toast.'

'That was a good sign.'

'Indeed. So I thought at first.'

What could the man mean? What had befallen Louisa? I had read of an illness, but little else, and knew not the outcome.

'The upshot of it was, she did little else but read the book, occasionally falling asleep for a period of rest. She was able to leave her bed, strong enough with the light food she was now accepting readily. She was still painfully thin and pale, but she sat in their drawing room and now and again made polite conversation when I visited. The doctor said she was regaining strength, and her wits also apparently, so my hope was that it would be as he predicted – that she would finish the book and forget the obsession that had gripped her. That damned book!' Deeves broke off and slumped back in his chair.

'So?'

His face wore a pained expression. He took a gulp of brandy before continuing. 'It was the doctor who found her.'

'Dead?' I know not what made me blurt out this most unmannerly question, but Deeves seemed to take no offence.

'Worse.'

'What is worse than death?'

'A living nightmare, man!' He threw the brandy glass into the hearth, where it shattered in a thousand pieces.

It took me some time to coax an account from him. It seemed the doctor had found Louisa sitting staring straight ahead, with the book closed on her lap. It was lying face down, so he concluded she had finally reached the end. For a while, he believed she would come to her senses as he'd predicted, but he could not have been more wrong. After some time it became apparent that the poor girl had lost her wits completely. When she did utter sounds they were strange. Deeves said they sounded like names, people and places, and there was great fear and wonder in her voice. The rest of the time she was a drooling wreck, unable to communicate or do anything for herself. Only the brief periods of dream-like trance restored her to some form of normality. But it was an illusion.

Now I knew the whole story. It was indeed tragic, and my heart went out to my old friend. But I wondered why, apart from sharing his grief with me, he had called me to his side. The reason soon became clear.

'I want you to read the book,' he croaked.

'What?'

'You are a man of logic and reason.' I nodded. 'You will not be carried away by flights of fancy as an imaginative girl would, or even as I myself might, with my sincere belief in the occult.'

I had to admit his reason.

'I need to know,' Deeves went on, 'if it was the book. If the book was the cause, or whether my poor Louisa was simply a victim of her own imagination.'

'How will I know?'

'You are probably the one person who is proof against the wiles of the book, as I understand it. If indeed it is as powerful as I suspect, you will detect its power long before it gains any control over you. Your disbelief of things magical protects you.' He gave a wry grin and dropped his gaze. 'I have no such protection.'

All of a sudden, he jerked his head up and fixed me with a burning stare. 'There is danger here. I'm asking you to take a risk, endanger your very soul, and all for …'

'For what?'

His gaze was steady, his voice soft now. 'All for the chance of bringing my beloved Louisa back.' The words came hurriedly. 'If I can find out the nature of the mischief that caused her condition I have ways of reversing the damage, I have resources.' The man looked desperate.

I felt no hope for him. But for his sake, I had to try. I had no fear of a book, despite the mysterious story Deeves had woven around it. In all my investigations, I had never found proof of the occult, of evil or magic, and did not think I was ever likely to.

Deeves had arranged for me to read the book for a certain time each day. The manservant would let me into the library and return when the specified time was up. He would accept no excuses, locking the library door behind us. In this way it was supposed I would be protected. From what, I did not know. Deeves himself would not enter the library, he said, for fear of being drawn in.

I had little respect for his precautions. In my own mind, I

was in little danger.

Certainly the first few sessions with the book seemed uneventful, and I may say, unexciting to the extreme. On first opening the book, I found the usual title page and flyleaf. Strangely, there was no author's name, acknowledgements or references. The story simply started: an innocuous tale of a young girl and a young man, a wicked uncle, and a quest.

It seemed at first a plain and unremarkable story, but as the days went by, I found myself looking forward to my readings, merely because it was a good story. I began to identify with the young man, the hero, as he won through many trials by his honesty and strength of will. I did have a nagging memory of Deeves telling me that Louisa had described a young woman as being the central character in the story. As this was clearly not the case, I put it down to her fevered imagination.

Each day, Deeves interviewed me about my reading. I recounted each episode to him after I left the library and he would make some remark or other. He homed in on the fact that I was becoming interested in the outcome.

'Perfectly normal for a reader,' I told him. 'It's an exciting book. Good plot, well written. It's a wonder it's not better known.'

Deeves shook his head.

Apart from our afternoon meetings, I saw Deeves only at dinner, and not always then. He spent much time at Louisa's house. One night he came home in a highly emotional state, bursting into the drawing room and pouring himself a brandy.

'What is the matter, Gerard? What has disturbed you so?

He paused a moment, then blurted out, 'They want to put her in an institution! A mental institution!'

He was distraught. I tried to calm him without success

and he retired to bed shortly after, taking the brandy decanter with him.

The next day, he was not present at our afternoon interview. It was a pity, because the plot of the story had become startlingly interesting. I had asked Coombes, the manservant, to leave me a little longer in the library, but he had been adamant. The cheek of the man! But he was immovable.

I was still angry when I sat for dinner, and my tone was rather abrupt as I addressed him. 'Where is your master, Coombes?'

Coombes lowered his head, as if confiding in me. 'I am not sure, sir, but I know that he is spending much time and effort to protect his fiancée from, er…'

'Being placed in an institution?'

'Precisely, sir.' Coombes did not even blink, and continued to serve the meal.

Over the next days, Deeves remained absent. Coombes did nothing other than open the library, turf me out at the appropriate time, resist my pleas and entreaties, serve dinner and refill the brandy and port decanters.

The story was now so exciting I was burning to know the outcome. I was that hero! I was doing the daring deeds that saved the maiden, beat the evil forces. It was a sublime and perfect story. How could the world not know of it?

Reading over the next few days, I suddenly became aware of a shadowy presence in the plot. My mind, afire and working at a supernormal pace, spotted him everywhere. No matter how many demons I slew, maidens I rescued, evil I conquered, he was there!

I dreamed of him. In my dreams he mocked me. I could not see his face, but I could feel his presence.

I checked myself. Was there any evil force at work here? Hardly. Yes, I was uncharacteristically drawn into the reading of a book. But what a book! I formed a resolution: this book would not be destroyed, the world must see it, as many people as possible must see it.

Deeves was still absent. Each day, I devoured the book voraciously, cramming as many of the words as possible into my hungry consciousness. Each night I would dream of it. I no longer asked Coombes for extra time, to be able to finish a chapter. No. That was too obvious, and he might inform his master, who would draw the wrong conclusion. I was not in the grip of any evil, I knew that. I had investigated such matters and the evidence was nil, zero. Instead, each day I kept an eye on my pocket watch and, before Coombes entered, would lay the book down with a considerable effort of self-will and compose myself. When he arrived, I was calm, composed, and unexcited, ready to leave and unruffled.

The dreams continued, now every night from the minute I fell asleep to the morning when I woke up. The shadowy presence was near, behind everything. I dreamed of striding to a corner, peering round it and getting a glimpse of him. But I always failed to do so. In my dreams.

Deeves returned. He told me he had finally conceded that Louisa should be moved to an institution. But to a private one of his choosing, where she would get the finest care and encouragement. He was still upset, but told me at length of his hopes for her and her recovery.

Everything was fine. I set to the task of presenting an amiable and stable appearance, calmly discussing his worries. No hint of my burning need to know the outcome of the story was apparent to my host.

Feeling secure and relaxed, and given Deeves' preoccupation with his fiancée, I foolishly ventured a question.

'Gerard,' I have now read most of your book. It is an exciting and involving plot, I concede, but evil? I do not think so.'

He looked up at me with attention.

'I have been here for several weeks. What I now suggest is you allow me to finish reading the whole book in one sitting and leave. I am absolutely positive there is nothing occult or untoward about it.'

For a moment, I saw acquiescence in his eyes, and rejoiced. Then, I saw him glance up, above my head, and I became aware that someone, presumably Coombes, was behind me.

'No!' and more vociferously: 'No! That is what she wanted, that is what destroyed her!'

There was no reasoning with him. He would not let me do what I wanted. He vowed to destroy the book the next day and ordered Coombes to make sure the library was locked.

I could not allow it. That night, I crept up to the first floor landing with the key I had purloined from the kitchen. Absurd! It was hung with all the others. I laughed at the foolishness. I unlocked the door, entered and locked it again behind me. By the light of the moon, I found a candle and lit it. The book was there, in its place. I hurried to the chair and settled to read.

In the story, His presence was stronger, I almost had Him. If I could find Him, I would win. I would triumph.

Deeves had, from the start, made me promise I would never read to the end without strict supervision. I was in turmoil. As I approached the last page, there was an overwhelming need, a burning urge to know! In my mind, I knew it would be foolish. I had set out with a plan. I was a man who followed plans. But surely it could not hurt …

I can hear the battering on the door, the shouts. Deeves is

pleading with me. But I am so near! I can nearly see Him! He is revealed. With the last words of the book, He steps out of the shadows. Around him is a crowd, a myriad of people, speaking in many tongues, begging and calling to me. I am overwhelmed. I hear above the clamour a woman's voice crying 'Gerard, Gerard, where are you?' Then I feel myself gripped, paralysed as He steps forward, filling my mind and my whole consciousness, and nothing else matters, nothing else is real.

I'd Like to Die in Spring

For a challenge to write poems about dying. This is one…

I'd like to die in spring
when summer's in the air,
and birds are on the wing
and new life everywhere.
… to die with dignity
in calm and gentle grace,
completeness in my soul
and warm sun on my face.

I'd like to die alone,
with beauty all around,
my head held in the air,
my feet firm on the ground,
while sitting on a chair
in a garden in the south,
and savouring the taste
of cherries in my mouth.

The path that I have trod
will end before the year.
I'd like to die in spring
with no regret or fear.

The Closing of the Year

And this, another …

I will not see the closing of the year,
Nor walk upon the land when winter comes.
Snow will not bathe me in its chilly light,
As I march onward to a fateful drum.

A kitchen with cool flinted walls and stove,
The Tuscan warmth of tiles that coat the floor,
My table bare and scrubbed to whitened board
With sunlight streaming through an opened door.

The air that wafts in, green and blossom-laved,
Fills lungs and heart with hope to drive out fear.
And in this summer kitchen where I sit,
I will not see the closing of the year.

Memoriam

What would you do? Nobody wants to be gloomy.

Tan slipped his ident into the slot. The big screen sprang to life and a deep voice boomed, 'Welcome, my name is Silas.' An oldish man with rosy cheeks, white hair and beard smiled out. Tan was pleased – he liked this operator. 'I have to advise you that our standard charges will apply. You've read them?'

'Yes, and I agree.' Tan spoke with care for the voice check.

'Good. So tell me, my son, what's the problem?'

'My father died.'

'I'm so sorry. You wish us to help?'

'Yes, if that's okay.'

'Excuse me while I check the records.' The screen blanked for a moment. 'Your last visit was eight months ago, so you're fine.' Tan relaxed – they kept changing the law.

'Ready when you are, my son,' the voice said gently. Tan lifted the silver helmet to his head.

It all came back. He recalled the hospital, the mind-numbing boredom, attempts at conversation as his father kept up a stream of complaint: nothing was right, from the doctors down to the woman who cleaned the floor. Tan was glad he'd been in there, he would have been unbearable at home. And it got worse. The illness took his dignity, and the smell … old age and death. He remembered his father's lined face, the pleading, pain-filled eyes that made him feel guilty.

Guilty! He'd paid for the best, hadn't he? Tan couldn't understand the ingratitude. When his father had finally consented to die, it had been a dreadful night: he'd clung on needlessly until the small hours. Tan was left to make all the arrangements for the funeral, having to be polite to grieving relatives who'd never visited his father in years talking about him as if he were a saint, not the whinging old man who had ruined Tan's life for the last six months. It was a really bad episode, which he could do without.

The operator's tone was businesslike. 'My son, thank you, I hope that wasn't too stressful. Would you like a snack or a drink while I prepare?'

'No thanks.' He knew better than to fall for that – the basic rate for the session was bad enough.

'Had you anything in mind?' The voice sounded less welcoming. The man was probably calculating his bonus. Tan did have one idea – it would cost, but this was to last him the rest of his life. He deserved some compensation.

'Yes, I was a watching a re-run of Mash the other night, and I thought maybe Alan Alda.'

'Good choice. I've several Alan Aldas. Would you like to view?'

'Please.'

After the adverts, several alternatives appeared on the screen one after the other.

'Oh, yes, the last one, definitely!'

'Excellent choice, my son, excellent.' The operator's tone was more than warm.

'How much?'

'Well, this is a premium product.' He must have missed the symbol. They had to show them by law, but these days they flashed past, or were hidden on a similar-coloured background. But it was good, and he'd earned it.

'I guess it's worth it.'

'You will not be disappointed.' Despite the operator's carefully-modulated tone, Tan detected a hint of glee. He mentally ticked off the costs. He could just about afford it.

'And would you like a vid for your family and friends? Your avatar is registered, so we can include you in shot, tending to him at the last, a dutiful son.'

'No, I don't think so.'

'Really? Oh well, perhaps some photographs?'

Tan looked away from the screen as the questions came. He'd heard about subliminals. 'No.'

'If that's what you wish, my son.' The face was smooth, benevolent. 'You know you can always come back at any time.' Yes, at extra charge. The operator didn't sound unhappy, so Tan guessed his bonus was safe. 'Please wait while I load your programme, it will only take a few moments. Just relax.' Tan watched the adverts as something clicked and hummed in his head. After a pause, the operator's voice spoke again. 'I'm pleased to say we're all done here now. Please take your mem-chip.' A small black square dropped into the tray in front of him. Tan took it reluctantly. He had to keep the chip by law. They checked. He was not able to remember what memory was stored, but it must be something bad. The chip would join the others lurking balefully in his desk drawer.

'You are advised to replay your original memory at intervals,' a voice announced mechanically. Tan smirked. And pay for a miniwipe? He didn't think so.

'Thank you for using our services. Please come back to me at any time if there are problems or questions. Have a good day my son and may only good memories go with you.' The operator smiled.

Tan slid his ident from the slot and the screen dimmed. He lifted the cap from his head and left the cubicle. A woman was waiting outside. As Tan stepped out, he held the door open for her.

'Who is it?' she whispered.

'Father Christmas.' They all called him that.

'I like him, except for …'

'I think he's just earned his bonus.' He caught the woman's expression. 'Don't worry, it was worth it.'

The woman smiled. 'Yes, it is, isn't it?'

His father had died, he remembered. He could see him now. The familiar face, twinkling eyes, lined but still young-looking. And his wise words … 'I have to go son, I love you, but I must help others now and go to meet your mom again. Don't worry, I'll be watching over you.'

Tan was happy, content. In his mind, Alan Alda's smiling face slipped into glorious death, looking tanned, fit and peaceful. Golden light crowned his head as he lay on a carpet of coloured flowers. Tan smiled. What a man his father had been!

The Day Peace Broke Out

Imagine if a peace broke out
In every town and neighbourhood
And that each person in their mind
Forgave the other, turned to good.
We'd then forget the old disputes,
Imagined slights and open wounds,
The thoughts that make you toss at night,
Wake with unease and give you grounds
For carrying on the spite and hate,
The blind dislike and threatened fear
The weakness of inadequates
And would it last a day? A year?
A minute or a second? Then
Someone would look and see a face
Expressionless, with absent gaze
And with a preconceived distaste
Assume it evil, bad or rude
And start again recycled hate
Pick on a tiny word or move
And we'd be back to present state.

and finally …

Now for the 'afters'. First, two of my very first pieces: one humorous, the other serious; one a poem, one a story. Just to illustrate my two extremes.

Then, a sample of my recently published humorous novel, Truckerson.

Thank you for reading.

Wanna See My Tits?

'What do think of them?'
She smiled,
leaning forward,
pushing them toward me.

I gazed at them.
'Nice,' I mumbled shyly.
'Nothing else?' She smirked.
'Well – they're plump.'
She swelled with pride.
'And?'
'They're very …'
I found another word.
'… perky.'

'They're very special, you know.'
I believed her.
We sat a while longer,

'Should I put them away now?'
She seemed disappointed.
I was bored.
'Well, they are lovely.'

I tried to show interest.
But when you've seen one pair, I guess you've seen them all.

contd …

She put the cage back on the table.
Looking grumpy.

The Boy in the Bus Station

The darkened windows of the brightly-lit waiting room were misted by the breath of the people crammed into its warmth. Every so often, a departure flashed on the screen, and travellers trooped out to board buses. New people crashed the doors open, breezing chill air over the toasting mass, puffing and rubbing their hands, welcoming the warmth within. There were all kinds: students, returning home for Christmas, elderly folks looking forward to family gatherings, lone men and women visiting relatives, and children.

Mary sat down opposite a harassed-looking man in a dark suit and long coat which hung open. Clutching her handbag, she settled herself and quietly examined him. Thin ginger hair plastered his scalp and the faint moustache on his upper lip twitched as he drew nervously on his cigarette. Beside him sat a boy. The boy wore a black quilted jacket. He was swinging his legs and banging his trainers on the steel frame of the seat. Mary decided he must be about nine or ten. He appeared ordinary apart from his eyes – darting, mischievous. The man's head turned to the boy. The banging stopped. The man gave Mary an apologetic smile.

'How old is he?' she asked, surprising herself.

'Ten, next March. He's my sister's boy,' the man volunteered. The boy stared at him. 'She died.'

'I'm so sorry.'

'It's been hard for him to settle.' The man glanced at the boy, who turned away, unreadable. Mary thought she was getting too deep in this conversation; maybe she should have been more cautious. 'The wife and I,' the man went on, 'we don't have kids ourselves, so it has been a bit of an adjustment for us. But we intend to bring him up right – it's our duty after all.'

'He seems like a good boy to me.' Why had she said that? Mary nervously awaited the man's response. The boy, seeming to sense her discomfort, grinned.

'Oh yes.' The man agreed. 'He's not a bad boy.' He was puffing frantically on the last of his cigarette. He threw it down and ground it under his shoe. Mary and the boy stared at it. Patting his pockets, the man rose. 'I'm sorry to ask this, but would you mind keeping an eye on him while I get some more cigarettes. I can't take him, it's a bar'. Mary nodded agreement, looking at the boy, who smiled directly at her.

'Come and sit here.' The boy bounced up, eyes sparkling, and crashed onto the seat next to her. 'Oh, you've a lot of energy!' she exclaimed as the steel frame shuddered. The boy's face became closed, eyes downcast.

'Sorry, lady, I'm sorry!' he blurted out.

'No,' Mary was repentant, 'I don't mind.' The boy perked up at once. 'Tell me what happened,' she asked. 'About your parents,' she added, catching the boy's puzzled expression.

'Oh! They both died. In a crash.'

'I'm sorry, I didn't mean to upset you.'

'How?'

She encouraged him to tell her more. He told her 'Uncle David' was looking after him. 'Do you like living with him?' Mary asked.

The boy lowered his head. 'They're very nice to me, I'm grateful to them. They have made sacrifices for me.'

The man was gone some time. Mary guessed more had drawn him to the bar than cigarettes. But she and the boy were getting on well. He told her jokes which made her laugh out loud. He became more and more animated, dark eyes twinkling as he teased and entertained her, mimicking TV personalities, and telling her about the things that had happened at his old school with his mates. They laughed together, as did others around, drawn by the boy's innocent humour.

'Wanna see me dance?' the boy exclaimed.

'Yes, yes!' Mary, clapping her hands, encouraged him, as did a few people nearby. The boy jumped up, bouncing with energy. He began to dance wildly, grinning all over his face. His whole appearance was transformed by his joyful grin and the sparkle in his eyes. Arms flailing in his big jacket, feet pounding, soles squeaking on the floor, twirling and bouncing, the boy danced. People gathered in a circle, clapping encouragement. As he danced, he laughed, and so did his audience. They chuckled, they looked at each other. 'Merry Christmas', some muttered, torn between a natural reserve and the happiness the boy brought.

'What's all this?' The man was back. The boy stopped dancing immediately, hanging his head down. 'Sorry!' he said.

'I should think so. These nice people don't want you making an exhibition of yourself and disturbing them. I'm sorry!' He smiled ingratiatingly at the crowd. Mary started to protest, but stifled the words. The bystanders melted away to their plastic seats in the warm room. Afraid to say too much, she watched as the boy slumped in his chair.

'Where are you off to?' Mary felt like a traitor, talking to the man. The boy sat, eyes downcast, silent now.

'Oh!' The man smiled. 'We're going to visit his grandparents for Christmas. Catherine wouldn't come: she wanted to visit her mother.' He glanced at the boy. 'I'm doing all this for him.' Later, as the man and the boy got up to board their bus, the boy turned and gave Mary an enormous wink.

Another year had passed. Mary sat in the muggy room with windows misted by condensation. It was that time again. She had enjoyed last year: the warmth and companionship at her sister's. For some reason, she thought of the boy. Unbidden, a smile rose to her lips. What a character he had been. She wondered how they were getting on.

The doors swung open. The ginger-haired man came in, accompanied by the boy, taller now.

'Hello!' Mary ventured hesitantly.

Recognition dawned on the man's face. 'Oh, hello! Funny this, meeting again.' They sat opposite. She tried to see the boy's expression, but his head was down. Noticing her gaze, the man exclaimed sharply, 'Say hello to the lady. Remember? Last year?' The boy lifted his head for a moment and gave a perfunctory greeting. 'Take no notice,' the man said. 'He sulks. Growing up, I expect. But he is behaving a lot better now, thanks to my wife's help.' The man gave a small shrug.

'Oh.' Mary decided not to pursue the conversation but after a while, the man leaned towards her.

'Er, excuse me, I have to go to the bathroom …'

'Oh, gladly!'

The man left, and she looked at the boy. 'Hello again!' she said brightly. His head rose. Where was the grin? 'Will you dance for me?' Mary so wanted to see that sparkle again.

The boy looked up. For an instant, she thought she glimpsed the life in his eyes. Then he dropped his gaze.

'I don't dance,' he said.

Truckerson

If you liked my poems and stories, you might be interested in another of my books.

Truckerson

ISBN: 1-906061-05-X

A sample of the story follows.

For details, see: www.e-griff.com

Truckerson

A 'lost chapter' of my humorous novel

It was a fine summer afternoon in the sleepy seaside town of Hastings. Along the parade a figure came into view. Just a schoolboy, but quite a striking one, probably a sixth-former. His bulky figure stood tall, his head set at a noble angle, chin high. His steps were steady, positive. He strode – no, he *marched.* A faint oompahing sound could be heard as his arms swung steadily as he progressed.

Barry Truckerson was remembering the year before when he'd met that chap Watson-something and the one he'd skimmed stones with – Barnes-Norris – funny how boffins all had double names. A lot of chums at school had, but when he'd asked Pop about it he'd just cuffed him gently and told him to get on with his prep.

He'd come down with his parents for a long weekend. They were staying at The Grand, which Truckerson had already decided wasn't very. But they'd been lucky to get bookings. It was the annual Boffin's conference again, as he liked to describe it to the annoyance of his father.

This morning, his mother had decided she wanted a new hat and Pop had taken her into the town. Truckerson could see the need for ladies to have new hats, but couldn't abide the process of acquiring them and tended to get rather fidgety sitting on a hard chair in some stuffy, smelly shop. This was unpopular with his father, so much so that he was prepared to sacrifice some of his hard-earned cash to keep the boy occupied. Ice-cream seemed to be a universal answer. After being instructed not to get into trouble, where not to go, and exactly when to return to the hotel for afternoon tea, Truckerson was released into the community.

The boy's dark eyes spotted the kiosk. As he approached it at a rate of knots, the woman inside smiled at him.

'Hello love,' she said. Truckerson wished sometimes ladies were not so familiar.

'A cone please, miss.'

'Oh, "miss" is it? Well I never …' The middle-aged woman giggled. 'Penny or twopenny?'

This was a fundamental test of Truckerson's character. His father admired thrift, but Truckerson admired ice-cream. 'Twopenny please,' he said firmly and clicked the coins down on the counter.

'Yes, I'd say that's right, for a big boy like you …' The woman glanced at him coyly, filling the cone. 'Would you like some raspberry on that?' The boy looked eager, then downcast. He had no more money, and it cost extra. The woman read his face. 'Oh, have this as a present, my dear.'

Truckerson beamed appreciation. 'Thank you very much miss, you are a very kind person.'

The woman reddened slightly, looking rather confused. 'Well I never … you could charm the birds from the trees, young man, there's some very lucky girls out there waiting for you.' She giggled again, girlishly.

Truckerson was puzzled, but also polite. With a small bow, he left the woman, wondering why on earth he should charm birds, and why on earth girls should be waiting for him. He strolled along, licking his ice. Women were funny creatures, he thought. In the sweet shop in the village where he and his school chums went, a new couple had recently taken over. The man was a gardener at the school, and his wife ran the shop. The other boys said she was really cross with them, but he'd always found her pleasant and friendly as he chatted to her and called her 'miss'. The man told him his wife thought he was 'a real little gentleman' and 'a handsome lad'. The other boys ragged him when they heard this, but Truckerson was more than compensated by an extra gob-stopper or piece of chocolate in his paper bag on a Saturday. He never said anything to the others as he scoffed them quietly.

As he walked, licking gently, he wondered about Germany. There was lots of talk of war – you'd think after the last lot, those bally krauts would have learned their lesson. But there was one thing he admired about them – marching. They were really good at that – he'd seen newsreels of loads of them marching all over the shop, all in step, wheeling and turning in perfect formation. One thing he couldn't stand was their arms waving in the air like demented trolleybuses. But for sheer technical skill, he did admire their precision.

Truckerson was well into the last third of his cone when he came opposite a beach shelter. He was rather startled to hear a man's voice shouting, 'Damn, damn'. He turned his head and saw a man sitting on the bench, looking down and banging his fist on the seat. Truckerson had never been one for bad manners.

'I say, sir,' he called out. The man looked up. 'That's bally rude if I may say so.'

The man appeared puzzled.

'I mean a lady or a young child might be passing and hear you swearing.'

'Was I?'

'Yes, sir, quite loud.'

'I'm sorry, I didn't realise.'

Truckerson realised the man was a gentleman. He knew this by his manner, and his genuine apology. But he wouldn't let him off that easily.

'You nearly made me drop my cone.' He gazed at the man steadily.

The man eyed the remains of the cone. For some reason he liked this lad, the set of his head, that open face with the dark dancing eyes. He could see the boy was wary but not afraid.

'What's your name, son?'

'Truckerson, sir, Barry Truckerson.'

'Well, mine's Whittle, Frank Whittle.'

After they had visited the kiosk, they both returned, licking their ice creams. Whittle glanced over at the boy. 'How on earth did you get raspberry?' he asked enviously.

'I don't know sir.'

'Are you a boffin sir?' Truckerson was not sure. After all, the man only had a single name. He wasn't sure if you were allowed to be a boffin with only a single name. But what else was he doing here? He wasn't a tourist and he was a gentleman, so he couldn't be a commercial traveller or anything like that.

'I'm an engineer.'

'Not a scientist?'

'Well, yes.'

Truckerson was puzzled. Could this man not make up his mind? He decided to change tack. 'What do you do sir?

'Engines.'

'What, for cars?'

'Planes.'

'Wow! I met an RAF chap here last year, sir he could tell an engine by the sound, Watson … something …'

'Watt?'

'What?'

'Never mind. Well if I have my way, engines will sound very different.'

'Why?'

'I want to make a new kind of engine. I'm not sure what yet.'

'Be good if they could get rid of propellers.' Truckerson said, idly licking his cone.

'Oh, I hardly think …' Whittle broke off thoughtfully.

Truckerson had seen a film where a man had been chopped up by a propeller – you didn't see it of course, just heard a horrible noise, but it had been pretty gruesome.

'I mean, couldn't they put them inside the engine?' Whittle was too polite to laugh. 'If they put them in the box, they'd be quieter as well.' Whittle searched for something the boy would understand.

'They wouldn't pull as well.'

'Make 'em faster then.' Truckerson spoke confidently, he knew that his Uncle Bertie's fan blew much harder if you switched it up a notch. 'And with more blades. And more propellers all in a row inside …' The boy was enthusiastic now, his eyes gleamed he gazed into the far horizon and a faint humming sound came from him. 'Whizzing round – it would go much faster, wouldn't it?' Truckerson knew from games that small things went faster than big ones, thinking of himself puffing round the track as young Nippy Johnston sped by.

Whittle could think of nothing to say. The boy was talking nonsense of course, but his head was buzzing strangely, buzzing with some curious ideas.

'And wouldn't it be like that fire hose thing?' Truckerson had recently decided to become a fireman. Although he had the introductory letter and the information from the Watson-something fellow from last year about the RAF, a temporary glitch in his career plans had occurred when he saw a film of fire-fighters at a big fire. It looked such fun! In one scene, a fireman had been thrown backwards by the force of the water when a hose was switched on.

'It's like a hose, sir, if you squirted the air out of a nozzle and revved up the fan, surely it would send the plane flying about all over the bally place?' Truckerson was waving his arms excitedly, forgetting his ice-cream, the last remaining lump of which flew up and landed on Whittle's knee.

Truckerson was immediately apologetic, afraid of what the man would say, but the man was quiet, ice-cream ignored, gazing out to sea. He stayed like that for a while, until Truckerson became somewhat concerned. His ice cream was sliding down the cone, clearly with the intention of joining Truckerson's.

These boffins, Truckerson thought, they're all the same. Queer blokes altogether.

He decided to start a conversation. 'Are you a marcher, sir?' he asked pleasantly, peering into the man's face. Whittle came back to reality with the boy's large face filling his vision. For a moment he was surprised, and hurriedly sat back.

'What? What did you say?'

'A marcher, sir. Are you a marcher?'

Whittle's face beamed. 'Of course, son, of course.' Looking down, he noticed the two blobs of ice-cream on the knee of his trousers. 'Oh dear,' he muttered as he wiped the cloth, 'we'd better get some more.'

'Rather!' Truckerson agreed enthusiastically.

As they marched together, Truckerson showed Whittle Watson-whatsit's 'oompah' trick.

'Brilliant.' Whittle said appreciatively.

They arrived at the kiosk out of breath and flushed. The woman looked at them curiously. 'What you been up to?' she asked, smiling.

'Marching,' they said in unison.

'Why on earth d'you want to do that? You boys, always playing games.'

As she cheerily prepared their ice-creams, little did she know that in just a few short years she would be thanking providence for the marching and marching-related abilities that would win the war for Britain. Yes, the Germans were fine marchers, but maybe their style was too rigid, too regimented? It could be that the more flexible and imaginative marching skills of the British would prove superior in the long term. Only time would tell.

'You've got raspberry again! Why didn't I get any?'

'Dunno sir,' Truckerson said sheepishly. Ladies, why were they so funny?

'Anyway, let me take your name, son. I'll write it down.'

'Why, sir?'

'Because …' Whittle's eyes fixed on the far horizon. Truckerson instinctively began to hum. '… you have given me a great idea, one that may help us win this war; one that may result in a new engine for our aeroplanes that will enable them to knock Johnny Hun out of the sky.' Truckerson's humming crescendoed as Whittle flung his arm upwards, propelling his ice-cream into the path of a passing gull.

'Hang on, sir. What war?' Truckerson stared at the man.

'Ah … Well, don't tell anyone I told you this, but it is likely we shall be at war with Germany again. It may be several years, but …' The man's head dropped, then rose again. His gaze bored into Truckerson. 'But with a generation like you coming along, we shall not want for brave men. It's you, son, and chaps like you who will save our country and keep it great!'

This was a turning point, both for Barry Truckerson, and the world. No longer did Truckerson wish to be a fireman. His resolve was set. He would join the Royal Air Force and become a flyer.

'I'll fly your planes sir! I'll whiz around the sky and knock the bloody Jerries for six!'

Looking at the boy's honest expression and keen, eager gaze, Whittle was reassured. The future was indeed safe. All he had to do was get the job done, and give this boy and others like him the tools to do theirs.

'I'm sure you will, Barry, I'm sure you will. Now, how about a march and another ice-cream?'

'Rather, sir. And … you can call me "Trux" if you like, all my pals do.'

'An honour, Trux, an honour. And by the way, never tell anyone what I said about the war or what we talked about, promise?'

'Scout's honour, sir.'

Truckerson arrived back at The Grand, late for afternoon tea, and curiously had little appetite. His father looked suspiciously at him. 'What have you been up to?'

'Marching, sir. And I met a man who makes 'plane engines.'

'Not another one of your "Boffins"?' his mother sounded amused.

'Yes, Mum. And I'm going to join the Air Force.'

'I thought you were going to be a fireman,' his father queried.

'Well, for a while, but now I see flying's what I want to do, really want to do. I'll be bally good at it.'

His mother shushed his language and looked around, but his father tousled his hair and said, 'That's good, son. I'm proud of you. We may need boys like you soon.' His mother gripped his father's hand and they glanced at each other. Truckerson felt they had some secret that he did not share. He suspected he had an inkling, but he couldn't reveal even to his parents what Whittle had told him.

The sun shone brightly as Squadron Leader Truckerson hauled himself out of the back of the car and greeted the assembled crew.

'So this is it, the top-secret plane?'

They nodded, and ushered him into the hangar.

'It's got no propellers!' Truckerson was surprised. Then he remembered.

'Who invented this?'

'Chap called Whittle, I think,' the Flight said.

Truckerson said nothing, remembering his vow of silence all those years before.

'And what's this?' There was a small plaque on the nose.

'Oh, it's a dedication to someone he knew, said he was instrumental in getting him to clarify the idea for it. Some chap he met at a conference once.'

Truckerson swelled with pride. Getting close and peering at the small, engraved plate, he read: 'Dedicated to the schoolboy who helped me achieve this: Harry Parkinson.'

Well, thought Truckerson, you can't win 'em all. I've learned a lot about history today.

And he had.

About the Author

John Griffiths is a retired business executive, who lives in the UK, and sometimes France, with his wife and dog. He has two grown-up children.

He is a published cartoonist and author, who began serious writing in his (early) retirement, and for a hobby, edits and prepares books for printing.

If you have any comments, or wish to see more of his cartoons or writing, you may wish to visit his website at:

www.e-griff.com

Other Popular Books from Grenadier

Frogs under the Wheels

and other tales

C R Krishnan

ISBN: 978-1-902000-01-5

With settings ranging from India to Brighton, these stories have a delightful humour and sheer humanity. Whether serious, light-hearted or sensitive, the author weaves a magic that is all his own. The introductions to each story are a treat: sharp and effective, often raising a chuckle in their own right. From a suitor clapping hands to ward of snakes and Narayan cheating Satan, to the Cessnas at Shoreham and the wife 'lost' on the M4, plus the amazing Frankie, these stories have something for everyone and anyone. Funny. Moving. True. And what is more, completely entertaining.

Available from Amazon and all good bookshops, or direct from Grenadier Productions and Publications, 5 St Helens Drive, Hove, Sussex BN3 8EA (www.grenadierpp.com)

Printed in the United Kingdom
by Lightning Source UK Ltd.
135880UK00001B/382-390/P